The SCRIPTURE READER

- The Tales of the Cartouche -

Soumeek Chowdhuri

notionpress
.com

INDIA • SINGAPORE • MALAYSIA

To
A couple of couples who have been true support to
me at different stages of my life
Souvik-Mahua
&
Choitali-Ratul
It is people like them who
have made
my books loved and appreciated at large.

Chapter 1

The sun was beating down hard, turning everything a reddish tint of beaten copper. In this part of the world the summer was aggressive, unrelenting, and unapologetic. Alekhya was paddling hard his bicycle up the slope. He was panting though he was young, fit, and strong.

They lived on a mound slightly above the rest of the town. It was three kilometers from the nearest bus stop where the bus that came and went twice a day dropped him from the district town forty kilometers away. In a country where public transport moves very slowly it is a good distance away.

The watch showed it was getting past five and yet in the summers it was still red hot. The shops were still closed, their shutters down. The afternoon siesta time for the shopkeepers. Alekhya had seen that the people of this little place were always more interested in comfort than success; an attitude he thoroughly hated. He had made no bones about it either. Always spoke his mind never mincing a word…something that never makes you popular though; people rarely like to listen to unkind truth.

He came to a stop outside his home; if such a place could be called home. Dilapidated, a tumbling small one storied house with paint flaking off its walls. No money to repair it, no one interested either. Their family was his mother and his old grandfather who was priest of the old temple on the mound. The small house and the two acres of useless land was the endowment from the temple trust.

He locked…double locked his old bicycle with a chain that was tied to the verandah pillar. Even an old bicycle had value to his family. They could not afford another. It was valuable to Alekhya till now, else he would be forced to walk almost two miles from the last bus stop, no mean feat in the heat.

The door and windows both made of wood were closed. That was not uncommon as the heat outside was unbearable. He rapped hard twice before the door was opened and his mother stood framed with terror on her face.

'Your grandfather is dying!'

He saw fear in her eyes, but was it fear for her own sake, Alekhya knew that. The old man who was her father-in-law was the only male member other than Alekhya after her husband had deserted her. She needed his support, however frail.

Alekhya rushed to his grandfather's room, more out of need to look decent than from any consternation.

His grandfather was lying in the huge old bed, a wasted little man, gasping for breath.

'Dadu! What is the matter?'

'Dadubhai…dadubhai… I never thought I could see you before I died,' the old man spoke in irregular gasps.

'Wait I will get the doctor…lay down quietly. Do not talk so much. Do you understand?'

'No, no its not required. I am already feeling better. The eyes showed that he had understood, though he did not say so in words, the old man was panting. 'It is the old malady, the asthmatic attack, it will go with my death when I lay on the brier bed. You need to give me your word, you will attend to the daily pujas in our temple, the God is our God, do not neglect it. It has brought you schooling, education and bought us food. What would have happened to us after your father never came back from the city. Else wrath may come upon us.'

'Well certainly I will, till I go to Kolkata, my results are out, I have been selected.' Alekhya spoke slowly letting the words sink in. He did not have too high an opinion of his grandfather's intelligence.

'God help us…now you dadubhai will go to the great city, study in the great university and will become a great man…our bad days are going to be over…bouma did you hear that? Bouma…'

'Take rest, I will shower and do the Sandhya puja.' Alekhya said calmly and came out of the room as his mother who was standing in the corner looked after him, she had hardly required calling,

Alekhya was sure she had been within earshot all the time.

It was a doleful look Alekhya felt. The look of one who is to lose something, her son, never to come back. Just like her husband. Well Alekhya knew she was mistaken; he was not one of those who run away.

***

An email printed from the only cybercafe in the area gave him the tangible proof that he had been selected for MA course in his chosen university, it had been his dream and it was being realized. It meant moving away from home but he had never been the emotional type, he wanted to see the world and this piece of paper with the print was the real thing, seeing is believing they say. Soon he was to go to the city he loved, Kolkata, learn from top professors, maybe one day hope to become famous. He was moving out of a small pond into the sea and the excitement was palpable.

Was this place worth living? People had of course lived here for centuries but had anything changed. No shops to speak of, no multiplexes or shopping malls, no he was not thinking of these things but today even in the twenty-first century when you had the bus stop almost two miles away and no transport to the place but a dusty road to walk on in the heat or take a shortcut across the fields, feet falling into potholes with every chance of getting fractured you hardly could call this living, this was to Alekhya dragging out an useless existence; a fact now more impressed upon him as he planned to move to the capital city for his studies.

He stopped at the tea shop which was his regular haunt. He wanted people to know the good news, we all like to do that when we are successful and Alekhya was no exception. People at the shop who all knew each other belonging to the same village were discussing about a political rally and rise in fuel prices. Cricket and the money they made in the local club tournaments was next in agenda, no one was in a mood to discuss academics or colleges. People are jealous, Alekhya knew that, well everyone did even if they did not accept it. People found it difficult to accept the truth. He bought a cigarette and lit it, and despite seeing one of his neighbors from the corner of his eye, continued to smoke it. Stylish rings he had seen film stars make in movies, he tried unsuccessfully but he continued to smoke in defiance to the neighbor who was ogling at him. Earlier deferent to him and his age, for it is a culture though now gradually extinct that people do not smoke in front of elders, he would have extinguished the cigarette but now the new Alekhya was no longer prepared to follow these rusted customs, he was shaking off the rust from every part of his being. Still, no one took much notice of him, something he could not fathom as it was not every day that people from this swamp, this village got selected to a top university like he had been.

Alekhya got up, he was disgusted with the place and with human nature, people seldom like to talk about things you like to hear, this was no exception but Alekhya unable to get anyone to discuss about him or the famous university he was going to was disappointed. He quietly left leaving them to their tattle and walked towards home. It was anyways getting late. He was going away from this place, surely to a place better than this, not knowing that story that many people believe Buddha to be associated with, having asked the traveler what type of people lived in the people in the place he had left and having got a reply that they were evil, wicked ones Buddha assured the traveler that the place he was moving into consisted of the very same type of people. Whether the great sage was associated with the story is unconfirmed, the wisdom of the story is indisputable.

The temple was old, no doubt over two to three hundred years but architects of the yesteryears had built these temples from red kiln burnt bricks as strong as stone. They had stood scorching summers, strong winds and were time tested.

If his grandfather had not fallen sick Alekhya would never have had to perform the job, he was due to do now. He was to perform the puja at the temple where his family had been hereditary priests for over two hundred years. Alekhya, a communist at heart who liked to call himself left liberal did not believe in God or pujas but a hereditary responsibility was something he could not deny. His mother had exaggerated, his grandfather was not dying but had been advised complete bed rest for ten days, his pressure had shot up alarmingly and he had had a blackout, the local primary health centre doctor who came only thrice a week to the place had examined him at home, a special favor extended to the village priest who still enjoyed some privileges in this old-world place. People usually knew which wheels were to be oiled to get the best results and the doctor knew if he did not upset the locally powerful his absence on the other three days when he practiced in the city would be blissfully overlooked.

The temple was on top of a small mound of earth and one had to ascend it by a flight of rough-cut stairs. The temple was visited by all locals and a steady income from the donations and offerings had given the family sustenance over centuries. One could not deny economic considerations even if they refused to accept others. Alekhya entered the temple, something he had not done since attending college. It was appalling, the state it was in, it smelt of incense sticks, rotten flowers, damp, ghee, and sour milk which were given as offering to the god. Cobwebs hung from every corner encrusted with reddish black dust. The light sieving in from the only little window was creating every possible design on the cobwebs.

Spiders ran across the place, but Alekhya was not put off, the temple garba-griha or womb house needed a spring cleaning. He always had phobia for dirt, had heard of some long name for it. Mysophobia was it? Or was it something else, he could not be sure. Often people rarely remembered these long words, and he had often wondered why people put in the effort to learn them.

He was going through it thoroughly and then it came to his eyes, under the disused registers that had been used over the years to keep records of all the donations that had come to the temple. The ones who had donated a lumpsum of money to have the memory of a loved one etched in stone on the floor.

A scroll of parchment, something quite stiff at least and covering it a sort of clay tablet, broken at the edges, reddish black in colour, which he had if he had not looked very carefully would seem like a part of the terracotta tiles that were a part of the temple. It was too dark here to see properly, using a bit of salu cloth to wrap the scroll and the clay tablet, Alekhya came out and locked the temple door. His spring cleaning was left unfinished. He went to his grandfather who denied having any knowledge about them except that he had been told in childhood about their wandering forefather who had brought it from somewhere in his sojourn in southern India, he did not know anymore or if he did, he had forgotten. What else did Alekhya expect of him in this poverty ridden old age, it was a miracle that he could say as much, there were many he knew, he said who could have only blabbered nonsense at his age. It was however from him that he had heard the stories, long winding ones of the ancestor as he had come to this place driven from the riches of the kingdom where the family had been traditional priests by invaders and new cruel rulers.

The story of civilizations are tales of men and women and yet they are more stories of barbarism. Throughout the world as his studies in ancient history had shown Alekhya that all the monuments which now were so grand in people's eyes were also monumental in their telling of exploitations, of slavery, of torture or extortion. Yet it was the monument builders, the kings that were celebrated over the ages rather than the artisans who remained an unknown unrecognized commodity, he felt himself let go of a sigh; he had always though himself leftist in his ideologies, what else could an educated young man be!

There was no point in haranguing his grandfather at present, Alekhya knew the uselessness of arguing with him, and taking the roll of parchment and the clay tablet wrapped in a red salu (a red soft cloth used for puja traditionally for wrapping articles used in puja), he went up the stairs to his own little room on the roof.

Chapter 2

On the roof was a little room. A 'chilekotha' or attic room. It was a room of his own. Alekhya enjoyed it though it was hot there during the day. His dreams spread wings there and took flight in the unlimited views of the green fields and trees waving and tossing in the breeze. It was the only place in that stifling house that Alekhya loved. It gave him a feeling of exhilaration, of freedom and freed him from the mundane.

He had hordes of books there, old ones belonging to his father and some old religious texts of his grandfather. He had devoured them all and got a good perspective he believed on ancient Indian theology and writings. He had to learn Sanskrit and Pali. He did it with diligence. The language in a country like India is diverse.

What little he understood because of his diligence was astonishing to him, though he understood only very little parts of it, the description he got from the words he had learnt told him this was a gold mine, his key to fame. Being famous is something we all desire but are loathe to accept, for fear that it might later be remembered only as sour grapes.

In number of notebooks, he noted down everything and tried to work out the hieroglyphic scripts of the Egyptians from the images he found on the internet. The only expensive thing he possessed was his laptop. Bought with the money he saved up from his scholarships and tuitions he gave to school children. He went on tapping away trying various permutations and combinations to break the code…no what he knew about these old-world languages was not enough it seemed. As an explorer requires direction, he thought he needed direction too. To have direction to put in one's effort is essential in any line of work- this was no exception.

Soon he was going to be a student in the top university in the state. He would learn from big names in the subject and then maybe he would visit the national library and museum and peruse documents and manuscripts to study and give him direction. He was lost in brown study when a shrill cry brought him to reality with a start.

It was his mother's voice from downstairs. He rushed down…something must have happened. Nothing much he found out to chagrin but that a stray cat had stolen the fish his mother had just bought from the market, it seemed too frivolous a cause to shout but then Alekhya knew well his highly strung and almost hysterical mother. Living on her own with an old man for her father-in-law and a small child she had gradually become like this.

Just as Alekhya was completing his packing his mother came into his room. She seldom did except to clean it.

'I have something to tell you.'

'Yes, ma.'

'You must always keep your mobile charged and pick up our calls.'

'How is it possible to always pick the calls, I might be in a class.'

'What is more important to you? Ma or classes?'

It was an illogical question and asked in the same vein, Alekhya did not reply. His mother continued.

'Your grandpa might fall ill.'

Alekhya would have liked to say that what could he do from being two hundred kilometers away but desisted. It would take the discussion on the same pathway, tortuous, illogical, and ultimately would end up with recriminations and unhappiness.

'Have you taken the charger and the money which I gave you?'

Alekhya nodded. When would him mother start behaving as if he was ten years old. He was twenty-two and going to do his masters for God's sake.

'Come down and have some food. Since you are going to college you seem to have changed. And now...'

Leaving the sentence unfinished, she turned without waiting for a reply and sobs were heard, muffled as she went down the stairs.

***

Arriving at Howrah station, the major junction for the metropolis Alekhya found himself jostling with hundreds of passengers who came from every part of the state to the city for bread, means to earn it and learning the ropes to eat it in future.

They were pushing each other to get out of the huge railway station. Alekhya had quite several bags and suitcases and he walked towards the taxi stand after asking the direction of a few people, his mother had told him only to take taxis from the stand for safety. A few drivers were calling him, giving out the fares. Alekhya ignored them. Touts and drivers abounded in this place.

Taxis were few in the postpaid part and a policeman was manning them. Alekhya stood in the queue behind ten to fifteen people, everyone was chattering at once, the out of line drivers still trying to wrench a fare from those who were sick, unable to wait or stand in the queue. It turned out to be a long wait. After waiting for thirty minutes an old ambassador car pulled up and the driver pulled a long face on hearing the destination which was just about five kilometers away. The policeman was moving on the vehicles with his lathi and Alekhya had scarcely loaded his luggage and squirmed into his seat that car started to move with a lurch. Soon he was passing an underpass with overpowering smell of urine and garbage and the taxi after negotiating the bend was on the beautifully lit Howrah bridge. What a view of the river Hooghly and all the tall buildings of the city! Alekhya was now in the city, a far cry from his rural haunts of Bankura. It was new life and new found liberation. Even in the stifling air, tinged with grime and smoke he enjoyed himself, it was the enjoyment of freedom, of living alone for the first time away from home.

Passing over the beautifully lit iconic Howrah bridge, Alekhya had the first glimpse of the river, Ganges, or Hooghly if one had to be precise though most called it the Ganges. The lights of the bridge or the buildings on the banks shone on the river face like a mirror and looked like thousands of fireflies Alekhya had seen in in village in the darkness, thousands felt like millions with his new eyes in the new city. There was a serene and somber quality in the dark waters of the mighty river that impressed Alekhya and since the traffic was slow he had some time to ponder over it before the taxi at quite a snail's pace crossed the bridge and entered Kolkata.

As the taxi wound along the road, crossing the BBD bag and strand road area, the wholesale market of the state and the area Alekhya saw shutters being pulled down and shops being shut, closing time after a whole day of gruesome dealings and sales.

The driver was taciturn and replied in monosyllables when asked something, the crux of the matter being that BB Ganguli Road on which the boarding house to which Alekhya was heading was one way and either he had to get down at the central metro station or pay twenty rupees over the fare if he had to make the detour via college street, Surya Sen Street and Amherst Street. Seeing the amount of luggage he had, Alekhya decided to pay the additional fare and in another ten minutes was deposited in front of an ancient, dark, dilapidated building which showed the words rainbow club, the boarding house.

***

Professor Tirthankar Bagchi was one of those rare professors who brought students to classes- a phenomenon rare nowadays. Bagchi's classes were well attended. His way of teaching was nice and graceful, his PowerPoint presentations superb. Civilizations lost thousands of years back came back to life and seemed to talk with his audience, it was a master's discourse and one that left a lingering taste like well brewed tea of the very best quality.

Alekhya had been simply blown away. He saw this man as his ideal, his hero. Worship often so ill placed was in his own opinion to be reserved for such brilliant people. The first class in which Bagchi taught and Alekhya attended stamped the greatness of Bagchi in his mind as a teacher. Could a teacher really weave such magic over mature post graduate students, mostly good ones too? It was a masters course class. Yet that is what Bagchi did. Civilizations and people from the past rose from dust in front of his eyes. A power point presentation and the lecturing style was pure magic. He felt like a fish who has been washed into the ocean from his little niche of a pond by flood waters, swept away literally by the waves. The flood of knowledge, of wit, of pure brilliance. He had gone to the canteen in the same mood and remained entranced, immune to the jeering comments by some of the city brats who were yet to accept the rustic.

A few boys were sitting in a huddle ogling at newcomers specially any good-looking guys or newcomers. Alekhya came within the radius of their gaze. One of them motioned to him with a finger, ominously as Alekhya knew. This call meant another introduction or intro as it was known in the campus. How many times would he have to say that he was not a city dweller, a top school pass out, that his father was no one big or that he had only come here to study and not do politics? These were the moot questions he had to answer in an obsequious manner, no rise of voice when the gore rose inside his throat, no reactions. Luckily, he had got a boarding house to stay, no not really luck, the reputation of this rather famous five-star university was not only for its academics but also for its ragging in hostels. It was rather more famous if so glorifying a word could be used to describe so infamous a process.

Alekhya meekly went to the table he had been summoned. He had no option, no one did have any option, the seniors supported by the union was too strong for any individual to defy at the initial stage.

It was the same rigmarole, the same charade, the same foolish laughter, no novelty, or intelligent questions or puzzles that Alekhya believed could also be called introduction or intro…neither was there any encouragement for studies, nothing except vilifying the professors or making caricatures of them…a sad situation if ratings of the famous autonomous university was concerned. Only one thing was common in this canteen with the tea shop he used to frequent in his village, idle gossip and no interest in others, people it seemed were the same everywhere, Alekhya ruefully thought he had not been fair to his village neighbors.

***

The boarding house called the new rainbow club was located on BB Ganguli Street as per the official address but its entrance was from a side lane, a small offshoot from the main thoroughfare. The entry door was between a goldsmith's shop and a popular tea stall. It stood, cracked walls, peeling paint from the walls a testimony to the times gone away. In the evening when all the shops were open and lights light, the glitter of glass, gold and the lights created an effect not only dazzling but unearthly quite in contrast to the narrow dark lanes that branched out from the main road. The boarding house which had about forty rooms, hundred boarders and only two toilets for each of the two floors was called mess in the colloquial term of Kolkata.

Alekhya had been given the address by one of his village kinsmen and he found himself entrenched in a double room with a middle-aged lawyer as his roommate. The lawyer as is often the case with them was ill informed and yet had a know all approach. On hearing that Alekhya had come to study history he let out a tremendous guffaw. What fool of a student would waste his time and money studying what was gone! There were so many new careers in computers and information technology or data science, quick job, and settlement. What could history give him but struggles, years of exams and even if he qualified them a government job. What made Alekhya think he could land one without connections. Did he live or in mars? Didn't he know of the thousands who had been duped for the job of schoolmaster. He himself was junior to a famous lawyer in the ongoing case in high court. Years of court battle and after winning the government would go to a higher bench or court and the candidates would be left in the roads drenched in rain and sweat and a million tears.

Alekhya of course knew all of this, the cases had come up in media several times, were hot topics in several talk shows on television but he did not dare to say that he was here for no schoolmaster's job. He wanted to become a researcher in history whose work would give new meanings to the history of India and would open avenues of understanding what and how the Indian civilization originated. The lawyer would only laugh and make worser comments besides thinking him to be a braggard. Alekhya chose the wiser path of keeping quiet.

His silence had better impact than any of his words could have had. Probably thinking that he had overdone it the lawyer mellowed down, no subject was bad if you studied well, Alekhya must do that and mind you no politics or girlfriends…the university was infamous for these, he had a responsibility for Alekhya and his welfare. His guardians had sent Alekhya here because he was staying there, he must remember that, not today but always and heed his words. Thus, having self-appointed himself as Alekhya's guardian, he took off his vest and bare bodied went to sleep, smelling of a mixture of sweat and talcum powder, snoring loudly on the adjoining bed.

Alekhya was left staring at the revolving fan in the airless room to contemplate his choice, both of his room, roommate, and career...ragging was not the exclusive domain of college seniors in canteens or hostels, it existed in various forms everywhere. Only it didn't get the same prominence it got when it happened in hostels.

Chapter 3

A morning spent in a boarding house colloquially called mess in old Kolkata would immediately justify it being named so. There were two toilets for an entire floor of boarders of really forty in number. The natural event in the morning when people had a rush could be easily presumed. Howls from the bathroom as cold water was poured over the bodies of people who had to do with cold water in both summer and winter were heard creating a strange cacophony. Somehow though it appeared quite impossible people managed to squeeze in and finally get ready, some for office, some for business and some for the colleges and universities, several being stone throw distance away from the mess.

A bare bodied man in a checked cotton printed loin cloth called the lungi was the most in demand. He was the oldest staff of the mess and knew all the boarders nearly ninety by their first names. Large steel plates heaped with white rice, hot from the oven with a watery dal and subzi or vegetables and fish curry came into the rooms of the boarders borne by this man day after day, year after year, a staple diet replaced by egg or chicken occasionally. Alekhya had already got used to this eclectic mix of people and the vagaries of these people. The youngest boarder to the oldest one, a college student of first year and a retired schoolmaster of seventy-eight formed this group.

Alekhya had on the first day decided to walk to the university which was no more than a kilometer from the mess where he stayed. Walking through the old by lanes of old central Kolkata was a pleasure to him. He discovered new shops, little nooks every day and somehow this walk drove out of his mind the milieu of the morning so he could concentrate on his classes. Little corners throwing up surprises at every turn, a dilapidated house with the broken cobwebby wooden khirki windows which when they were scrolled up would let in the rays of the sun decorating the floor and walls in myriad designs.

Shops old and moldy with shopkeepers who seemed even more coated with mold, the very spirit. Yet there were happier faces, thoughtful ones or if Alekhya thought correctly worried ones. Business was not easy to run these days and if one became invisible and watched the full exchange of goods or money at these places, there were millions of such places, one would become worried too.

He turned the final corner and entered a narrow lane; it was one on which an ancient and famous medical books seller had its shop. The shutters were being just rolled up by the employee but there was already a small crowd outside the shop. Alekhya often wondered for he was now a regular traveler by this route, why the customers presumably medical students who knew the opening time of the shop came in before time. Maybe medical students just loved to read and loved to run the race, the rat race where no one wants to be left behind. He had reached the main road and turning right after a few hundred meters reached his college gates.

***

The boys and girls who were dressed up in expensive dresses, cut a different figure to what you expected in a college. They were from rich families and it was somewhat of a mystery to Alekhya that still a large percentage of rich kids seemed to make it to the top universities or colleges in every stream. It was not that being rich prevented you from being good in studies or talent needed to make it to these places but it seemed a bit unfair to Alekhya that talent and brains just like money had gravitated to the rich but what he was blissfully unaware of was that money could buy you the best coaching, the best teachers and that could often compensate for what little deficit there was in natural talent.

It was here that for the first time that he saw her. There was no name at first. Just she, glowing like amber in the sun, not too fair but a beautiful face and superb figure. That is what attract people at first though they say that beauty is only skin deep. Priya, for that was the name Alekhya heard her friends call her by was awestruck and bamboozled.

He stole sidewise glances, a bit timid and shy of the smart Kolkata girl.

Fate has strange things in store for us, he met her in the bus stop. Priya was waiting at the bus stop waiting for her bus while Alekhya had some things to buy from Shyambazar, a new bedsheet and a pillow. Number 78/1 was a frequent bus and they did not have to wait long but Priya smiled as she saw him getting up too. The bus was relatively empty in the late afternoon at college street and both got seats. As the bus wound its way through the crowded Bidhan Sarani more people started getting on and soon Alekhya could no longer see her seated in the ladies' seat on the opposite side. Shyambazar came and Alekhya got up to get down, did he mistake it or was Priya trying to dodge several bodies and looking at him too. The conductor was shouting at the top of his voice and he was hustled off the bus. He turned his head to look back and met the gaze of Priya looking intently through the window.

***

The roommate Alekhya had in his double room was a lawyer and a middle-aged man. The man had a family and a flat but had a room in the boarding which was centrally located and easily accessible from any point in the city. He loved the light wholesome meals and the snatches of sleep he could catch there in between meeting his clients. His court was close to the boarding house. He snored loudly whenever he slept which caused Alekhya tremendous irritation and disturbance but the man was genial, look a kind brotherly interest in Alekhya and was away in the nights when he went back to his family leaving Alekhya with the solitary use of the double room. Having a single room or a small flat was beyond his modest means and compromise as is often the case had to be made with the circumstances, beggars could not be choosers.

***

The presiding deity of the boarding house was a lady everyone barring the older members called auntie. She was the owner of the house with a dead dog and husband for memory and running the boarding house was her solitary occupation now. Once, Alekhya had heard someone say that the lady had been in a receptionist in a large private hospital and her efficiency had translated into running the boarding house where most things were maintained better than one expects in such a decrepit house. From the very first day she had taken a fancy to Alekhya and his meals often carried a bit extra on account of this. He paid his rent on the third of every month, kept a respectful manner and never forgot to switch off his light and fan while he stepped outside his room, all facts observed by both the hawk-eyed owner as well as the closed-circuit cameras that were almost omnipresent. It had put him in the good books from day one. Money paid right on time and good habits as the world perceives them go a long way in creating an impression in the world.

Alekhya had just started to smoke and it was new habit which seems to grow upon us faster than we think. He now was still in that mode where people avoid smoking in front of their elders in Indian culture. Searching for a nook out of the vigilant eyes of the cameras and the boarding owner, he found a small corner, but soon the stub ends of cigarettes other than the brand he smoked and burnt matches showed him that other people knew of this before him. Nothing in the world you find is original.

***

Priya was amongst those people who remain standing out even though there might be a crowd. She was slender, fair and think black hair which was coloured a hue of dark electric blue, quite an attractive colour if one had the other assets. Priya had them, in plenty.

She was the central flame around which there were lot of moths hovering around, most dancing to their deaths. Alekhya watched her warily, not being of the same upbringing or background. Priya absolutely ignored him, too enamored by her bunch of admirers. She had been brought up as a single child by a single parent, her mother who was a working lady. It was difficult often for her to attend the guardian's forum meetings, which was commented on by the others.

Shreyashi Banerjee had been called strong by all who knew her, whether as a matter of boosting her mental strength or just routinely is not known but Shreyashi was strong, it was always said. The problem with these types of epithets is that you cannot any longer show your weaknesses, your vulnerability so to speak, she could no longer be herself. She drew herself into a cocoon, a shell out of which no one could pull her out.

It was always the guardian's meeting that caused a bit of disquiet in her mind. That was the day she felt ill at ease, right from the morning.

Priya needed her at that meeting, one parent and that too not strong enough to bear the cross would never do, it had a detrimental effect on the mind of the young and she would feel guilty if that happened. As usually happens when we really try to be punctual, she arrived much earlier than the hour of the meeting at college street. Seeing herself well ahead of the schedule she decided to indulge herself, a dab sherbet at paramount, it had been one of her favourites during her university days and then to the book shops, she had always loved books and she sighed when she thought of it, she was destined to work in a reputed university having the caliber and the grades necessary and more, but...but fate had dealt her a cruel hand, though it had been masked by a glove, well no point in thinking these things now, but mind was a thing that often did not listen to us. She looked at the wrist watch, a smart watch she had gifted herself, almost four. She took a couple of books she had selected, paid, and moved swiftly down the stairs and out into the street, thronged with booksellers, prospective buyers and hordes of others who seemed to have no business.

The meeting would have started, she always liked to slip in a little late, unobserved and into the backbenches.

Chapter 4

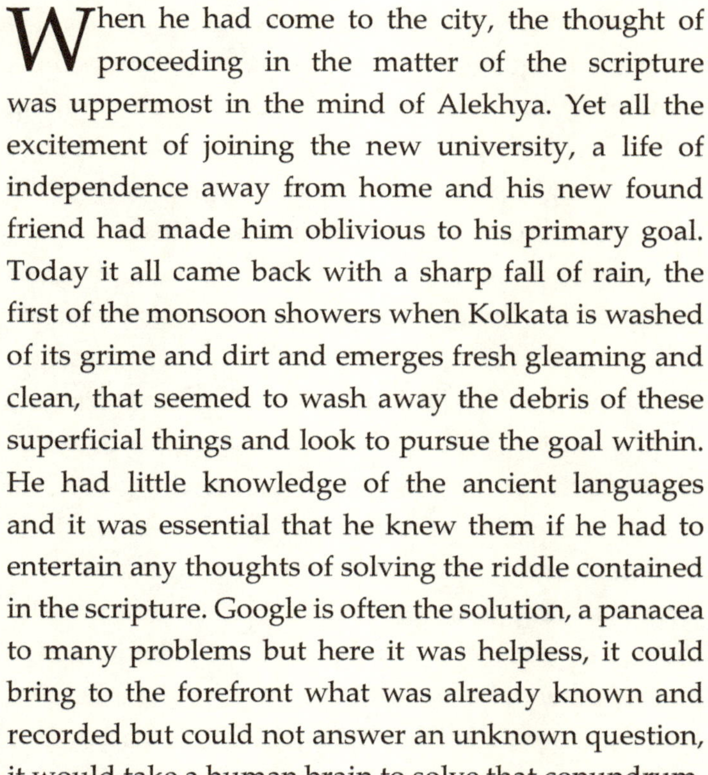

When he had come to the city, the thought of proceeding in the matter of the scripture was uppermost in the mind of Alekhya. Yet all the excitement of joining the new university, a life of independence away from home and his new found friend had made him oblivious to his primary goal. Today it all came back with a sharp fall of rain, the first of the monsoon showers when Kolkata is washed of its grime and dirt and emerges fresh gleaming and clean, that seemed to wash away the debris of these superficial things and look to pursue the goal within. He had little knowledge of the ancient languages and it was essential that he knew them if he had to entertain any thoughts of solving the riddle contained in the scripture. Google is often the solution, a panacea to many problems but here it was helpless, it could bring to the forefront what was already known and recorded but could not answer an unknown question, it would take a human brain to solve that conundrum.

The language in the scripture appeared to him somewhat like Sanskrit and somewhat like Pali, the words having a pronounced effect on so called words in the Dravidian language, akin to those words used in the Aryan texts, a clear linking or usage of various words between the two so called disparate civilizations. But all the history books had put down the Dravidians as ancient races somewhat inferior to the Aryan races, a thought that had been passed on for generations, imbibed into the society and carried on by many even in the contemporary age.

If the languages were linked so could the people, something that could turn out to be a revolutionizing in the annals of history and could bring about a change in the thought process of the country; not easy in the political environment but possible nevertheless.

Language is a mode of expression of one's thoughts, the living world and even nature seems to have a language. When man came into existence, did he have a standard language of communication? Does it exist even today? Did not same words mean different things in many cases across the globe. He knew that signs and pictures had finally been distilled to letters and words and then language had been formed during natural evolution. Had the Aryans who claimed to be the purer race developed the language that was then taken on and modified by the others? A language as pure as their lineage? Well, he had doubts and he meant to solve it.

His first resort was the retired schoolmaster in his adjoining room. He had heard someone say that he had been a teacher of Sanskrit in school and a great pundit. In life what we hear and what we know are often vastly different things. He was soon to receive another proof of this, the schoolmaster it was true had taught Sanskrit, but it had only been in a primary level and his knowledge in the matter was sketchy at best. He directed Alekhya to visit the National library and the museum after peering through his thick glasses at the cover and pages of the scripture. They were vast storehouses of knowledge besides having a few knowledgeable people.

He knew one of them by name and thought maybe he could help him if he really wanted. He was however quite scathing about the ability or wish of the current students to pursue anything with diligence. He scoffed at him. Alekhya did not say anything but did decide to go with the advice of the master. His reading would go places if he got to the library and was able to harness its riches.

***

The national library was one of the finest buildings Alekhya had seen, white, palatial and with its huge collection of books quite out of the world. They were going to a new building soon he had heard and Alekhya thought it a shame that someone could think of using these modern iron cement structures, blobs of ugliness he thought them and desert the antique palace like structures of dreams. Still day after day the world went on like this and more and more noble buildings hit the dust. He had a reference from the retired school master and he first went in search of Nripenbabu.

Nripenbabu, one of the most senior of the library staffs to his great dismay, he found out was on leave and would return only after 7 days after a family occasion. Alekhya was disappointed and his face must have shown it, the staff at the counter asked him

'What is it you want? Are you a member of the library?'

'No sir.'

'Then it is better you take this form, fill it up and get it signed by your institute. It will take some time by which your Nripenbabu would be back.' The man at the counter smiled as he said this, it seemed to transform his face, how a smile transforms people Alekhya had often wondered.

'Thank you, sir,' said Alekhya taking the form eagerly. His time would not be wasted. He put the form in his backpack and came out. A bus took him to the nearest bus stop from his boarding house. It was nearing evening time and the lights of the jewelers were coming on, it was an ethereal sight, the glint of glass, metal, and the myriad reflections that they cast seemed to transport Alekhya to a different world; one in which there was only glitter and gold. Well, it was not true, Alekhya knew that. These very streets and lanes were the vilest when the shine and glitter had been taken away.

He entered his room and almost immediately his roommate the lawyer came in too.

'Are you up to some secret treasure hunt?' Asked the fat lawyer in mock seriousness and then he roared with laughter at his own joke.

'Well, there is no treasure hidden except in films my boy, better start reading, you are going to find it hard to find a job if you do not have top notch results, all these job scams now are in the headlines. I am junior to one of the most revered names in the high court in one of these cases.' he added with importance.

Alekhya gave no reply but continued to pore through the manuscript and jot down words or signs he felt he needed to know to proceed in the matter. The words of his roommate had no effect on him.

Grumbling as he got out of his official gown and coat, the lawyer went to the bathroom failing to have any impact on his audience. He poked his head into another room and passed some comment and Alekhya heard another roar of laughter.

Chapter 5

We all yearn acceptance, acceptance of the society and acceptance of the peers makes us do many things that we otherwise would not have done.

It was payesh his mother cooked from the best Govind bhog rice and milk from the local dairy with almonds and raisins, the payesh full of them as he loved them. But today it had been different. The puja that his doddering grandfather offered for him specially on this day was replaced by painful bumps on the backside. Birthday bumps were the city friend's way of wishing him happy birthday. It was painful but what of that, his friends were pleased and that is what mattered most. He had decided to make himself one of them, transformation from the rustic Bankura boy to the suave smart guy of the urbane. He was fair, slim, and attractive, so why not!

Birthday bumps and smearing of cakes on face more than what people ate was their way of enjoying the birthdays. It was not that he liked it too much but one often had to make the pretense of liking and that itself was often greater than liking itself. His friends had all flooded the social medias with those pictures and he was feeling happy, an empty happiness it was but happiness nevertheless.

***

Bus stops have had their role in history as lover's spots all around the world. In countries where there are more people than space to be private sometimes new spots get quick popularity. But some spots still retain the old-world charm; Bus stops amongst them. Alekhya had met Priya for the first time at this bus stop and time had stopped for him as it does for those when in love. Of course, they realize the folly of this in later life often but to accept it would be to accept one's foolishness; not something we are very comfortable doing. We all try to prove ourselves smart, in the end making a fool of ourselves often but it is a habit that dies hard.

The meeting had turned into more meetings and then into small chats and short conversations before turning into love at full bloom. It is easy when you are in your early twenties.

Alekhya believed in the old style of love instead of the newer trend of lovemaking, the bit of mystery and purdah proving more intriguing than being disillusioned when the veil has been completely removed. Was he a male chauvinist? Well maybe he was. These meeting turned into a routine.

One day they could not get into the bus, it was too crowded and decided to make a break journey to the music school by metro and then by foot. That was first time they went to a restaurant together. The famous hundred-year-old Niranjan agar on the central avenue adjoining Girish Park metro. The century old restaurant, famous for its egg devil filled with minced meat and duck egg, a whole one between which the minced meat was sandwiched and fried in a crispy batter. Priya had never eaten here and Alekhya had come once with his friends, it was a gourmet delight. Only more delightful when you are with people you like, often love.

***

Shreyashi started to worry about her daughter once she started getting late on a regular basis, it was always the start, wasn't it? The avoided questions, the diverted gaze, they were quite definite signs. She should know going by experience. But she was the modern-day mother or rather wanted her daughter to believe it. She avoided asking questions which could embarrass her but she was a mother after all and she was anxious, anxious about the mistakes girls make at this age, the mistake she herself had done. It was quite common.

***

There was no power in the village, a storm a day back and the area would be out of electric supply for a couple of days. It was routine and quite accepted part of the life that went on in the village in remote Bankura even in the twenty-first century.

Alekhya's mother was sitting in the kitchen stirring a pot of payesh, something she always made on Alekhya's birthday. She had made pulao and chicken hoping that her son might pay a surprise visit on his birthday, for two days the mobile network was down too and her son might have called. She held hope, that elixir that gives us power to bear the difficult and the unpalatable times.

Now as the evening advanced and her hopes dwindled, there was time for the last bus yet, she mused as to what Alekhya must be feeling with no call from her grandfather and mother on his birthday. She comforted herself saying that Alekhya must be very busy with his studies. She was proud of her son, inordinately proud but she was also afraid. The demons of her husband never coming back and gone missing among the millions of the great city was at the back of her mind.

Her father-in-law was calling, she hurriedly put down the pot from the stove and went to him.

Late at night when Alekhya did not arrive or even call, she ate a small morsel of rice and threw away the delicacies she had worked so hard to prepare, a stream of steady tears falling from her eyes.

Chapter 6

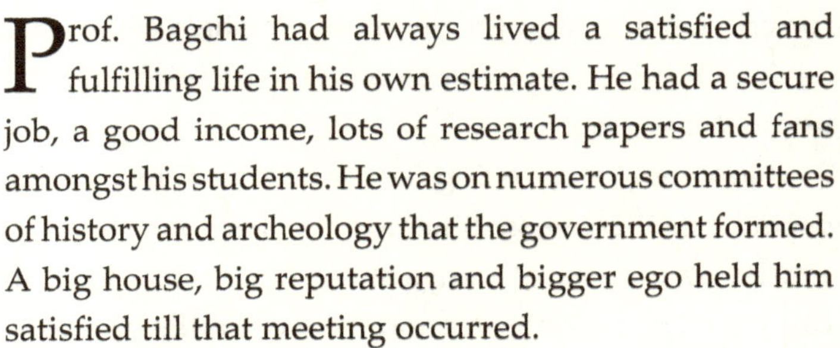

Prof. Bagchi had always lived a satisfied and fulfilling life in his own estimate. He had a secure job, a good income, lots of research papers and fans amongst his students. He was on numerous committees of history and archeology that the government formed. A big house, big reputation and bigger ego held him satisfied till that meeting occurred.

He had never however tasted originality or understood its addicting power till then. Alekhya like a gust of wind had brought it into his life and he had been blown away though he had been forced not to show it. The discussion had lasted less than an hour but it had been very different.

Alekhya had been shy, almost diffident in approaching him. But finally, he had done and listening to what he had to say in the corridor Bagchi had scented something worthwhile to invite him to his house. He was not known to be too friendly with students so it was a rare exception. Alekhya maybe would arrive early. It often was the case when people were eager, as the eagerness died down, they seldom arrived on time…

A find of a kind, an interpretation of an ancient scripture. A new civilization drawing light, it could prove to be a coup. A special one for the sake of his career. He waited for Alekhya to come feeling an excitement he did not feel for many years.

***

Often when one tries to be punctual one often ends up being early, it is something that occurs universally. It happened to Alekhya too. He ended up reaching the professor's place by 12.30 when he was to have reached by 1 pm. Hesitant to ring the bell so early, he still had mortal dread of the professor, he walked up and down the little tree lined lane and even smoked the cigarette he often did when tense, it was a habit he had recently acquired to appear cool to his classmates.

At the stroke of one, he rang the doorbell. There was sound of footsteps descending the staircase and the professor opened the door himself. The student had expected a lesser person, a servant or a maid and he was somewhat surprised.

The servant's gone out for some sweets the professor said in reply to his look rather than to any words, he had spoken none. Every moment he felt awed by this man. Intelligent, graceful yet so detached, aloof to the common world at large.

'Come in my boy, make yourself comfortable' said the professor leading him to the huge living room, old, classy, aesthetically decorated with old world décor. 'What would you like to drink? Please do not hesitate.'

Alekhya felt shy, the famous professor they saw from the distance on the glittering pedestal showing such humility and warmth. We feel the warmth of famous people than we feel the same in case of those who are not.

'Anything will do sir, a cold drink...' he left the sentence unfinished.

Scarcely had he consumed the cold ice lined thums up, Alekhya was asked to go up to the study. They shall require some books the professor said. the professor led the way to the first floor up a flight of rickety old wooden stairs that spiraled up. It was a separate staircase that led up from the ground floor to the study, an isolated nook. The house though old, Alekhya noted was well-maintained, marble statues adorned the landings.

They entered a huge room, lined with bookcases on three sides, the musty smell of old books greeted them. It was a smell he loved, a smell of books.

'Sit down' said the professor indicating a chair opposite his own at the other side of a huge mahogany desk. Alekhya felt intimidated by the place, the thousands of books, the ancient mahogany desk, and the picture of a double-whiskered man gazing malevolently from the frame above.

'This belonged to my grandfather, you see here' pointing the malevolent man in the picture.

'Now show me what did you want to show to me. Have you got the scripture?'

Alekhya timidly took out the scripture from his backpack and handed it to the professor.

Taking it and unfolding it from the red salu cloth he studied it under a powerful lamp.

After about fifteen minutes of minute examination the professor looked up, his eyes were shining.

'So, this belongs to your family?'

'Yes sir.'

'Do you understand the meaning of the writing?'

'Not the whole of it, just some parts sir.' Alekhya was cautious.

'If this is an authentic document and you can read it properly it can be quite interesting. But most of the language, its old Pali and Sanskrit from what little I understand. But most of it is to be deciphered, it is in a language older than either of these languages. We need to go back more, but I am not an expert in languages. Have you thought how to go about it?'

'Sir, I am going to the national library and the Indian museum. I have got some help from both sources and have started to decipher them, started to read them. I will show you a few examples.'

Alekhya took out a hardbound notebook from his backpack and started explaining to the professor. For the next four hours two heads and backs were bent in intent study of the notes Alekhya had made.

'Soon I will have someone who can help me have a start.'

'Hmm, come back to me after you have made progress. Call me first before coming.' It was clearly mentioned and subtle indication that he was welcome only when the matter was progressing.

Chapter 7

Nripenbabu was back and Alekhya gave him the retired schoolmasters name. Squinting heavily as if trying to remember, Nripenbabu finally connected the memory and got talking with Alekhya. He first got the membership form and handed it to the card section for further processing which Alekhya had finally got signed from his institute after much haggling.

'You can come anytime you please and study here. Here is the main section which will interest you. You will get your card soon.'

The library was so huge that everything seemed dwarfed in comparison to it. Alekhya being one of the regular visitors, Nripen babu knew him well now. Nripen babu had worked in the national library for twenty-five years yet rarely found readers who were regular. People like the weather now everywhere was fickle, they came in for a few days and then went missing. Alekhya was one of those exceptions. He was young too, not more than 21. He had an idea not altogether wrong that the young rarely read nowadays. He was on the lookout for rare books, mythology,

Indian history, cryptology, books only scholars would be interested in. Nripen babu followed this boy with some degree of interest in the time he was not busy at the counter.

***

The books he had got from the library opened new vistas in front of him. They were like magic lanterns lighting his way as he bored deeper into the tunnel of this mystery. Truth has attraction and itself is more beautiful than any picturesque landscape. He read up on the Indus valley civilization, the great mysteries surrounding the writing on the pottery and seals found in the digs. All about the attempts to decipher it. A recent paper in the famous journal Nature showed him some key words that could link the Vagai valley civilization with the IVC. The digs at Keeladi had thrown up some fresh evidence only some years back.

If only he could use these words to form a cohesive whole a key which could form a solution to the mystery of the Dravidian and the Aryan races. It was always supposed, that the Aryans had developed the civilizations in India, all the thoughts came from them, all development came from them, now if something came up to upset the apple cart it would not be easily accepted by the semi-Aryan society the northern parts of India and its fringes.

Sometimes as Alekhya thought about it, he felt an inadequacy, he belonged himself to one of these races that was non-Aryan in a way. If he could change the thought process by a discovery, if he could think about it. He started with the word as had been mentioned in the research paper, the tooth word. As Alekhya studied the papers and compared them to the language of the scriptures, he found some similarities which could not be completely overlooked. The language was somewhat like Sanskrit and to some extent like ancient Pali but not like them exactly.

The signs and words had pronounced effect of these Dravidian words, Pali, Pallam but the problem was the linking of the two. The Aryan languages that were spoken in the civilizations that had a predominant Aryan influence could be spoken by the Dravidians too if they had inhabited these areas but why was this scripture that had been brought from the south of the country bear a similarity to the Aryan languages, what could be the bridge of connection. It had always been a tendency of the country to look down on the Dravidians as somewhat interior to the Aryans, a lower caste or race, all school books, history books spoke in that tone from time immemorial. If now this scripture spoke about another civilization that was in sync with the Indus valley civilization a lot of thoughts had to be revolutionized. But it was a bitter pill and not something everyone could swallow. Alekhya was aware as everyone else of the domination of Indian politics by the northern people, the right-wing politicians would not take too kindly to the suggestion. The political environment in the country was at its most polarized state from the very time of independence.

However, all this was only conjecture till he could prove it conclusively. If he read this scripture properly, he could be the pioneer, but he needed support and funds and all the authority that was needed to go ahead. First things first he drank a glass of water from the tap and sat down again to meticulously read and interpret every word. It was back breaking work but he was starting to see light at the end of the tunnel. Now it was only perseverance that could take him to his goal.

Chapter 8

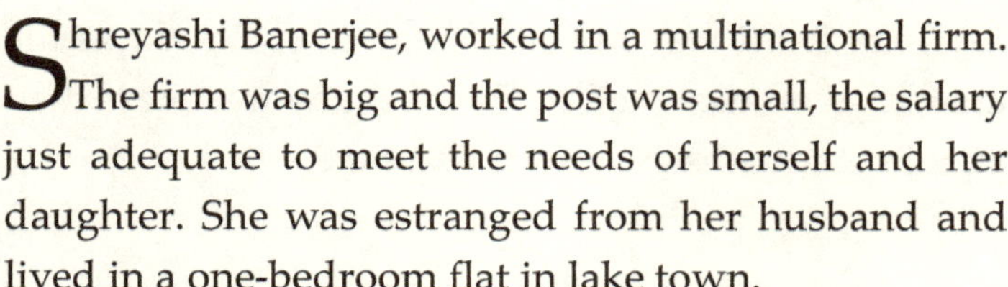

Shreyashi Banerjee, worked in a multinational firm. The firm was big and the post was small, the salary just adequate to meet the needs of herself and her daughter. She was estranged from her husband and lived in a one-bedroom flat in lake town.

She had never separated from her husband officially and never asked for any money; hence the small flat was all she could afford. Her daughter was now in college, a top one which required a high fee too.

She had kept the knowledge of the father from the daughter, the identity had never been discussed. She only knew her father did not live with them. But one promise given to herself had to be kept and that time was drawing close, the eighteenth birthday of her daughter was approaching and she had decided her daughter was to be given a free choice as to whom she chose as her guardian in adult life. There were many advantages her father could give which she could now never dream of giving. Yet if she had been allowed to pursue her career, she would have been in the same position too, now it could never be. She sat down at her computer and started typing out the letter, a letter nowadays was a novelty yet that was the only way she could convey her feelings and truth to her daughter. It was timed exactly to reach her daughter's mail on her eighteenth but at the night, after the festivities were over. She didn't have the heart, yes, she still had it though she did not wear it on her sleeve as they say. The heart was meant to stay deep inside as the anatomy had designed it. The birthday was more than couple of months away, she had time.

***

Duttagupta, the principal curator of the museum had dozed off. A stomach full of rice and shady cool room were good preconditions for an afternoon siesta. He now had little interest left in his job which was now no more than just a means of livelihood for him.

He had once been a keen historian, archeologist, and scholar but years of rotting away at government service had taken away what was good and left him what was ruin of a noble man. Recently his old urge to study, to probe the unknown, to know the things that were hidden in the dust always sort of intrigued him.

He had gone through the number of old issues and volumes and they were lying in a heap face down, some dog-eared. There was a knock at the door.

'Come in'

Alekhya stepped from the shadows into the lighted room.

'Oh, it's you. Come in.'

Alekhya had still not shaken off his nervousness fully and he stood with his hands crossed in front of each other.

Duttagupta gulped down a glass of water, sit down my boy. I have something here for you. He turned a thick old notebook, dog -eared and turning the pages carefully as if they were made of old parchment he came upon a page, adjusted his glasses, and started to read.

'I have here references from a very famous journal published internationally, it argues a very interesting point. Every language has some key words, they continue to remain unchanged when taken on by other language civilizations, a non-borrowable ultra-conserved vocabulary item. I will give you an example, tooth is such a word. It is a part of the Swadesh's list of the culture free non borrowable basic vocabulary list, on number 43 of 100 such items. Here is the list, I have a photocopy here for you. Start with this and analyze the scripture, you will see new light.'

He stopped as if exhausted from his unaccustomed habit of hard work.

Alekhya was excited, he had now something to work upon. He had already taken two dictionaries from the library, the Tamil, and the Brahmi, he knew Sanskrit well, right from school had a very good foundation in it. So, he did not need a dictionary to read it.

'Sir, can you just see what else can help in my researches?'

Duttagupta handed him a volume. On the cover of the old book was written Leipzig-Jakarta list for glottochronological analysis around the world. No one seemed to have read or borrowed the book much since its inclusion in the library archives.

'Thanks a lot sir, I will come tomorrow with what I find.'

Duttagupta nodded; he seemed already dozing off. This job had ruined him as a scholar and made a permanent employee of him. He did not seem to have that essential element; energy, to pursue a work. He had grown fat on a fatter salary and lost it in the maze of service, something that often has the knack of doing this to many.

Alekhya, was young, energetic, and ambitious. He set off for his boarding house armed with the books and the printouts, it was going to be a sleepless night for him. He had a mystery to crack.

***

Memories are good, memories are bad and often memories are painful. The painful memories persist the longest, they linger on creating an ulcer, a malignant one often that bores into the very core of mind. The photograph she took out of the locked chamber in the almirah, was one of those painful memories. It was in sepia, a tint that makes things very poignant, often much more than they really are, or does it?

It was a picture of herself, youthful, good looking in a bridal dress. It was the "sindoor-dan or vermillion marking" of the bride by her husband, there are so many marks that are indelible, she did not know if it was not one of them but undoubtedly it was significant in the life of a Hindu woman. She could not forget her roots. There was cattle branding done, well she could not think of this derogatory and non- sensical things…

She started composing the rest of the letter, more anger, more vitriol, more unpleasant truths a little more coloured than they had been, anger does colour them in a hue of red, a dusky angry red. Her daughter must know everything, Shreya Banerjee was immovable on this point.

Her hands swiftly moved over the keys, typing furiously. Anger, more anger and now her skin was flushed a dark red.

***

Alekhya, was sitting cross-legged on his bed. A small folding table on the bed supporting his laptop, a pile of books beside him. The mobile internet connection was slow in his room which being a very old building had very thick walls. He had bolted his door so that he could work in peace.

In finding out the meaning of the scripture he had to depend on the dictionaries, some words archaic might be found missing but a picture could be formed if he was diligent enough. The Tamil Brahmi script he had tried to work out and now was doing a decent job of it. This scripture was a part of the so-called Sangam literature, a conglomeration of poets of Tamil origin who had described in detail the civilization in the south India at its seat near Madurai between 4th century BCE and 2nd century BCE.

He read the description and matched them to the words he had learnt from the dictionary; he had always been good with languages. The description of the area was clear from a river, in probability Vaigai, the now almost dry river that runs near Madurai. Also was clear the connections and trade relations with other regions and countries.

The recurrence of the words like Pilu, Piru and others that Duttagupta had drawn his attention to, Alekhya saw a clear connection between this lost civilization and the Indus valley civilization. Both were almost co-existent. The thought that the Dravidians had no urban civilization to speak of while all the development had come from the Indus valley followed by the gangetic plains seemed to be challenged. Only if they could find a connection to the IVC, it could be present in the pottery shred but it had no definite source reference and could have come from anywhere. Its presence with the scripture did not mean they were to be considered from the same source, the little inscriptions showed an uncanny similarity to the potteries and writings found from the Harrapan civilization.

He started to read the scripture more minutely, he needed to know some points from which the location of this civilization could be traced. The broader picture was emerging.

***

Duttagupta was lying in bed, a single bed lamp was on and the semi darkness showed the massive shape of his wife, snoring and asleep. He was reading a transcript from Hiuen Tsang's travelogue he had got after much search from the archives. The ancient city of Kapisa of the indus valley was rising in front of his eyes and he was discovering his old love for reading. Pilusara called Siang-Kien in Chinese Siang meaning elephant, the elephant mountain, the local legend relating the mountain to a spirit which took the shape of an elephant, the spirit showing loyalty to lord buddha. Thus, again was the proof that pilu must have been used as an elephant word in Indus valley civilization regions of Afghanistan since antiquity.

He from his vast reading of the yesteryears was aware of the 6th century AD inscriptions found from western india like the Sankheda plate of Santilla and the Svamiraja's Nagardhan copper plates which contains the official designations of Mahapilupati and Pilupati meaning great master of elephants. His convictions were becoming stronger, he would speak to Alekhya about this next day, how that boy's eyes shone, he loved it, his old self rediscovered. He switched off the light and tried to sleep, not an easy task when you had a snoring machine beside you, he lay down resignedly with a sigh.

Chapter 9

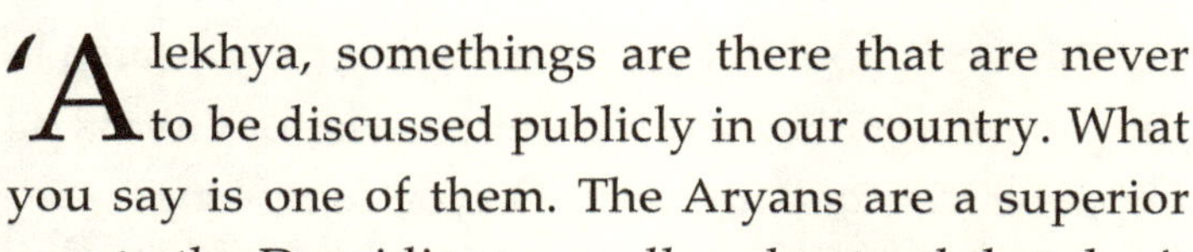

'Alekhya, somethings are there that are never to be discussed publicly in our country. What you say is one of them. The Aryans are a superior race to the Dravidians, we all understand that don't we?'

'Sir, what is the logic behind this?'

'The Aryans were the ones who developed the civilizations, from them people learnt the skills of civilization, the languages. They were the driving force, you have written this article in completely the opposite way, and I fear it may draw some serious censures from the authorities if it came into print. I cannot allow it.'

'But sir, I think there are proofs to the contrary.'

'What brought you to such a foolish conclusion? Will you come out with it, all your questions I remember now regarding these topics, I had always wondered about the reasons. Come clean my boy and I will think about it.'

Alekhya came clean, at that age you do not think twice of coming clean or hoping that the world was clean.

'Just see the words here sir' Alekhya said pointing to a heavily scribbled page in the notebook. 'The word for elephant is Piru in the Mesopotamia bronze age, ivory has been called Pirus in Persian documents come from the word pilu, a proto-Dravidian word for elephant. The Mesopotamians and Persians who traded ivory and elephants from the Indus valley civilization got the word from them. It is etymologically related to the proto-Dravidian word pal and its various forms pil or pel which stand for tooth. Do you follow me?'

The professor nodded slightly; his head seemed to be swimming in the sea of etymology. It was not his subject but he could see the dim outline that was being formed.

Alekhya's eyes were shining like points of light or probably it reflected the lights in the room.

'There is further evidence, the toothbrush tree-Salvadora persica that tree characteristic of the Indus valley civilization, it abounded sir, forests of them, huge clusters whose twigs were used as toothbrush from time immemorial. Now come to the Mahabharata, that great reference of the Indian civilization. The description of Aratta as a place where forests of pilu trees stand and those five rivers flow; the Satadru, the Vipasa, the Iravati, the Candrabhaga and the Vitasta with Sindhu as the sixth. Can it mean anything else? I ask you to disprove it.'

The professor was now himself in a maze of thought. The logic was bearing him down like a stream, strong, gurgling, energetic, bound to and determined to have its way.

***

First child birth is always difficult. You are inexperienced, in most cases ill-informed and in a lot of anxiety. Yet her husband who had much to her chagrin and deepest dissapointment left her one week before the expected date of delivery for a training in Delhi. It was very important for his career, his career when he had irrevocably damaged hers without turning a hair, made her pregnant much against her wish and put her in this position. Her in-laws were not to arrive till the end of the week, which meant she had to do all the household chores herself and suffer the pain alone. Every pang of pain made her wince and feel even more nervous than before.

How she hated it! Her husband, her in-laws, and that child unborn sometimes for having taken from her everything she had loved. Her studies, her opportunities, even her looks and made her look like a sack of flour. Self-reproach took the place of anger sometimes; she deserved it having loved. Love was always a pain and she well knew why now, all too well.

The words came gushing out like the liquor amni that had leaked just before someone from an adjoining flat took her in an ambulance to the hospital, she had uttered a terrible cry seeing this blood red fluid come out, what else could she do? The person had come from the adjoining flat, he never had spoken to them.

He had been kind in his own way, much kinder than the man who was responsible for this though both were men and this one unmarried and good looking too. All this she came to notice and know later. She was in mortal terror and pain and so she remained till the baby came out causing even more pain, tearing her insides after a few hours. Shreyashi had paid in full, as she had heard the great poet write, the debt of love.

***

Alekhya continued. 'See here sir, I have the reference, no less that the Swadesh's list included directly in the Leipzig-Jakarta list. It is a part of the culture free non-borrowable basic vocabulary list, it is the 43rd item', he pointed to the printout Duttagupta had given him.

'All this clearly points to the fact that the Dravidians must have coexisted as a civilization as developed or more than the Indus valley people. Why else borrow words from their vocabulary? I mean to get to the bottom of this but I will need your help. The scripture talks of a place in the Vaigai river valley in southern India, we need to trace the place organize an archeological dig and unearth the truth of this civilization. The Keeladi expeditions are the beginning but this is much more extensive. The very roots of our civilization will be questioned. Just let me finish the scripture reading, it will direct us to the place.'

'What help do you need from me?'

'Sir, it is not easy to organize an archeological expedition. I know that, only you of all people I know can help me and do this.'

Chapter 10

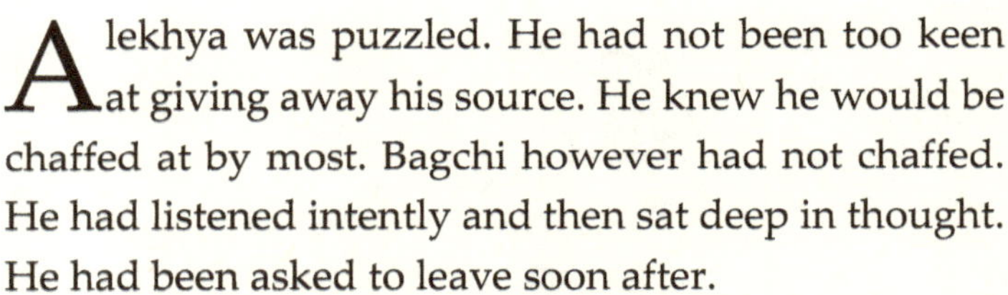

Alekhya was puzzled. He had not been too keen at giving away his source. He knew he would be chaffed at by most. Bagchi however had not chaffed. He had listened intently and then sat deep in thought. He had been asked to leave soon after.

The tea that they had got used to having together had been forgotten. Bagchi had not asked and he did not have the temerity to suggest. He still was afraid of Bagchi, afraid was the right word. We often replace it by softer words, kinder words respect, reverence but the real word is fear, that is what often guides us in our actions.

Fear can often lead to various actions otherwise not commonly done; it is a very good stimulant in more ways than one. Alekhya was no different to other people. He was now afraid. What he had thought could work out, there was a wild hope that it would and on the other side was an anxiety that it might all come to a nought, the fear of failure and more importantly the fear of ridicule.

Chapter 11

Professor Bagchi had been in a state of excitement from the day he had heard all of Alekhya's arguments, he had not accepted them of course but he was excited at the prospect. There were two vital parts to this, one was the cartouches were what Alekhya thought they were and the second if the first surmise was correct was the possibility of persuading the ASI and the government officials about the archeological expedition. He was aware of the reservations in such cases for the expedition and the cost of it. A sanction would not come easily, he was sure of that fact.

Professor Bagchi always had a roadmap in his mind, it was this planned approach when many far more talented than him had fallen behind and he was quite proud of the fact. He started by trying to approach Dr. Ramanan, the deputy director of ASI and more importantly very intimately connected to the top brass in the corridors of power. It was he who called all the shots at ASI while the director was more of a figurehead. It was no easy job to get in touch with the man.

He was always at symposiums or trainings or some conference. The message that would come back was "I am in a meeting I will call you back" would never happen. He was a small man, his stature in the field was mainly by oiling the right hinges in the administrative machinery. His projects never lacked funds or were held up due to permissions, anyone in the circles of the ASI knew that. The government was quite amenable to his wishes.

Bagchi who had been well acquainted over years to the functioning of the ASI knew he needed Ramanan's nod and blessings. Ten minutes he had to wait on the line only to be told by Ramanan's secretary that he was still on the call, it was better he called back after 1 pm. Bagchi put down the phone, he was irritated but not disappointed, he had hardly expected to be attended by Ramanan on the first attempt. He was knowing how these people loved to keep up their image of importance often pomposity. He would try again and again till he succeeded.

***

Bagchi was sitting with the laptop in the executive lounge of Kolkata airport. He was intently studying a presentation that he had assiduously prepared. This was his key to opening of the excavation grant, though Ramanan had been non-committal, the government was not too keen on opening any pandoras box. It could lead to many questions not all easy to answer.

Ramanan had however granted Bagchi an audience at Delhi in the department in presence of a few deputy secretaries based on the preliminary report which Bagchi had sent him.

The flight was slightly delayed which made him tense, he was to meet the top brass at 4 pm and it was getting on to 11 am. The rescheduled flight was at 11.30 am, rather cutting it fine. Bagchi was confident he would cut a good figure. He was brilliant in presentations and it was always his best chance when people allowed him to talk.

Putting some fine touches sipping a cup of black coffee, Bagchi knew he had a chance, that was all that he needed to push open the door.

***

It was a late-night flight that was bringing Bagchi back from the capital in turbulent weather, two lurches already in the first fifteen minutes of being airborne. The bureaucrats as was expected had not given him a go ahead, they had however not stopped him which was a good sign. They wanted more substantive proof, and Bagchi had been asked to go to the spot where the pottery shred and manuscript had come from, Bankura, a place remote and almost unknown to those in the corridors of power.

It meant travelling to the village where Alekhya claimed the things were kept, he wanted to be sure that this was not some sort of a hoax, a wild goose chase based on a young student's assumptions. Bagchi was never fond of air travel which seemed to him unsafe being suspended at over thirty thousand feet in this small metallic contraption, the floorboard underneath his feet just too fragile, it had always seemed to him, it was rubbish, of course he knew he was safe, millions flew everyday around the globe but it was an obsessive thought he could not somehow manage to rationalize with, he was irrational when it came to this, all human beings at some point are irrational, some accept it while some do not.

The plane bumped as it fell into an air pocket, once more shaking up the rational roadmap Bagchi was making in his mind. He now just wanted this flight to get over…

Chapter 12

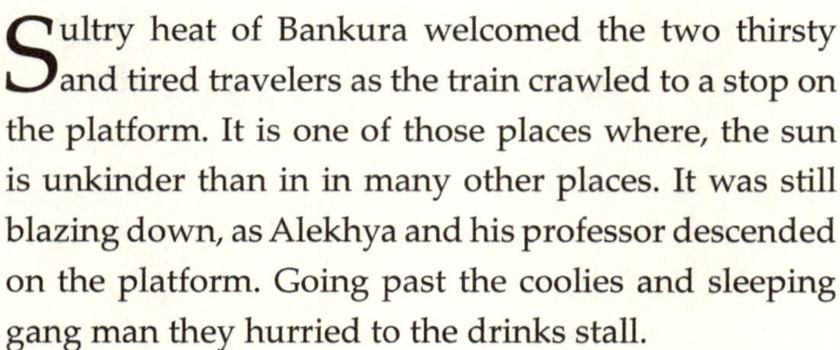

Sultry heat of Bankura welcomed the two thirsty and tired travelers as the train crawled to a stop on the platform. It is one of those places where, the sun is unkinder than in in many other places. It was still blazing down, as Alekhya and his professor descended on the platform. Going past the coolies and sleeping gang man they hurried to the drinks stall.

'A coke for me and seven up for sir, its chilled right?'

'Two hours no power babu' said the shopkeeper showing his teeth.

The coolish soft drink was gulped down in no time. They badly needed it.

Picking up the professor's suitcase and putting on his own backpack Alekhya started walking towards the toto stand, clamoring drivers and rickshaw pullers shouting at the top of their voices for their gullible prey.

Sidestepping them tactfully Alekhya hired a toto from the outside of the station as they often took less charges and was greeted by foul language from the toto drivers standing behind.

'How far is it?'

'It's about half hour from here to the bus stand.'

The professor audibly groaned.

Soon the toto bypassing the rickshaws and autos and walkers who paid no heed to the honking of horns reached the bus terminal.

Number of buses were parked and there were small goomty like counters for the tickets. Alekhya was sure it was like a deadly furnace under those tin goomties.

Having expertly got his tickets from the sweating guy in a vest who was the conductor too, both window seats Alekhya returned.

'When will the bus leave?'

'Well sir, its due at 4 pm but it has not arrived yet.'

'But its nearly 4 now.'

'Buses seldom run-on schedule here sir, often they are late, frequently very late.'

'Oh my god! What a god forsaken place'

'It was your choice sir; you were adamant on coming yourself.' There was a slight irritation in the student's voice. He had not been too keen on taking the famous professor to his dilapidated home, we however poor all like to keep up appearances.

The professor remained silent.

The bus finally started, or rather moved as it had seemed unable or unwilling to do so for quite some time. Laden with vegetables and vendors who had come to the town selling fish, vegetables and what not from the various surrounding villages it was a feat that it moved at all. Heat, squalor, smells of every type mingled with sweat pervaded the interior too on an airless sultry day. Stopping every yard, as it seemed to the irate professor, it finally got to the open roads where though the heat seemed less stifling there was no breeze. After two hours of this hellish drive, they arrived at the native village of Alekhya, a small backwater situated in the backdrop of a few small hillocks, very little greenery and a lot of red soil that seemed to coat the very scene with a tint much like rust.

***

After they had bathed in the open with cool refreshing water from the well, the professor could hardly wait before he was taken to the temple where the Sandhya aarati was being performed with lamps. Once over he was all over the place scarcely waiting for the devotees to disappear. He was all impatience, and satiety could only be obtained by seeing everything from the "garba griha" to the old box the things had been brought, from the lands deep south by the ancestors of Alekhya.

Only after he had retired to bed after a long rendezvous with Alekhya's grandfather post dinner could Alekhya's mother talk with him. She had been waiting for this opportunity and accosted Alekhya just as he was about to go to his roof top room.

'Who was this professor Alekhya was so gaga about?'

Alekhya gave an expansive description of the illustrious professor, a little more embellished as we are all apt to give when describing someone, we are crazy about. We paint them in vivid and brilliant hues which even the very best hardly deserve.

What was it to do with him and what about his classes and studies and exams, that was what he had gone to the city for, wasn't it? What was his plan for his life and career when she her mother was working like an unpaid slave to save a few rupees for his studies.

Alekhya, young, arrogant, and brash in his dreams of success gave a very loose and grandiose reply. He was not mediocre. What did his mother expect of him? Was he to live the life of mediocrity that most were destined to live due to lack of ability or industry. He was not short of either. He would be famous by the time others barely passed their examination. He would be celebrated across the country and this expedition that had almost been sealed now was all a result of ingeniousness and if he was right in using the word, brilliance. He had torn the secret out of the heart of a clay tablet a few thousand years old and deciphered the meaning of the scripture which would now lead them to the archeological site that could throw a new light on the whole Indian civilization. Wasn't that the aim of any historian worthy of note, of any archeologist asked Alekhya.

Bamboozled by the degree of knowledge his mother whimpered that she hoped her son could become a famous and great man, that would be the highest culmination of her years of toil after his father had disappeared after going to the city to seek out his fortune, maybe God had finally looked up and taken pity.

Alekhya had no time for the sentimental rubbish as he often called it behind her back. Asking her not to worry, he was old enough to take care of himself and his interests he went up the stairs and slammed shut the door of the chile-kotha, the rooftop room, half afraid that his mother might follow up upstairs.

***

Bagchi lay in the bed drenched in sweat, it had been a hot day and the ceiling fan was doing nothing to drive away the heat of the night. These districts in the western part of the state were always so hot in the summer months, an almost unbearable stifling heat lay like a blanket on the hot night, almost asphyxiating the people in its folds.

His trip however had not been in vain. He had got what he and of course the Archeological survey wanted. He was sure now of the authenticity of the claim that Alekhya had laid, of the originality and antiquity of the scripture and the origin of the pottery shred.

Taking him to be a worldly man, the old man had spoken his heart out to him.

The great grandfather of the old man (of course he was an young boy then) had told him of the travels of his ancestors, they had belonged to a race of traditional priests who had once worked under the Sangam dynasty down south, where they had been trusted and extremely prosperous but good times and luck do not last forever and there had come a day when their lords had been driven out and before the doom, the ancestor had been asked to go to far off land where the sacred pottery and scriptures could be kept in safety. He had travelled north east finally reaching the place which was then quite inhabitable.

The professor thought it still applied to the place but for the sake of peace and garnering further information kept quiet.

The garrulous old man went on, how it had all happened, how they had built up their reputation, how all their riches were looted by the dacoits that infested these areas then, the professor had no interest in all these unnecessary details and hardly listened to the recital though he kept the mask of being a sincere listener.

It all now came back to him in the middle of the sleepless night and as he prepared of turning this tale into a brilliantly packaged presentation, he knew he had a chance of a lifetime here. Confident and quietly proud of his powers to impress and carry off the grant he lay on his side and despite the heat was soon asleep.

***

Alekhya's grandfather prided himself as a good storyteller. He could make a story believable in way great writers and artists of oration do. There remains no difference between truth and the make believe. Of course, what he had told his grandson's famous professor had been the truth but he had embellished it with a bit about the riches. Emile Gaboriau had somewhere spoken of the power of the tongue enhancing a fact to three times its actual length and though the old man might never have heard of the great French writer, he was doing only what writers base their wring upon; a study of human character, broadly the same globally.

He had assured the professor of the authenticity of the manuscript and the antiquity beyond reasonable doubt and was quite sure that the glory of his forefathers would be reignited by the expedition that his grandson was undertaking with the professor.

Chapter 13

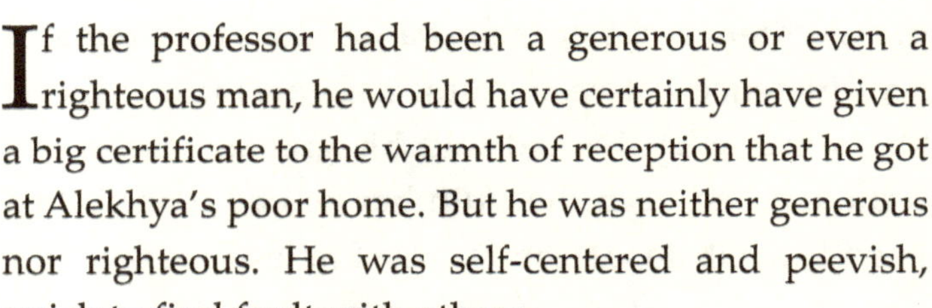

If the professor had been a generous or even a righteous man, he would have certainly have given a big certificate to the warmth of reception that he got at Alekhya's poor home. But he was neither generous nor righteous. He was self-centered and peevish, quick to find fault with others.

Alekhya's mother delighted with her son coming home after months and accompanied by his illustrious professor from Kolkata had cooked up some special delicacies. Moong dal with fish head, rohu fish kalia, mutton fresh from the local farm and the whitest rice greeted them at dinner.

Alekhya's grandfather though bed ridden and failing in health tried to keep up a conversation with Bagchi; he was after all his grandson's professor and their guest.

The discussion went to the scripture and the pottery shred, the point where it came into the family and the place where their ancestors or someone from whom they had obtained the scripture had written in the scripture about the details of the event. The language was a very old Sanskrit Pali or something akin to it.

Alekhya's grandfather did not have much education. He only could mumble some little-known folklores prevalent in the family about the scripture. The shred of pottery which was in the temple and regular pujas performed as God was the important part of this visit. The inscription he had seen on the shred was in an unknown script, one not known but somewhat like the script seen in antiquities obtained from the Harrapan mounds, this Bagchi was now getting more and more sure of, the source of this scripture and the pottery piece now roughly located to the Vagai valley as the place had been a small village twenty miles from Madurai, the seat of the Sangam civilization. This made sense as the Keeladi excavations had shown. There was every chance of a new finding since they were closely related areas, but the scripture had indicated something that was new, the Harrapan connection. If that happened, well that was not to be thought of, even history has its makers and well, he had an early morning class and the flight to Chennai and flights worried him.

***

'Right bro, you are off to a real expedition.' Arpan looked excited.

Alekhya smiled; it was the smile of the winner. Four of them who were a close gang in college were sitting in a pub, drinks on the table. Alekhya was giving the three Arpan, Prithwish and Priya a treat. He was due to leave next morning for Chennai and he wanted to give his friends, his sweetheart Priya included a treat before he left.

'Here we are poring over the books and notes and here's our Alekhya off to do archeological expeditions, what a difference' said the slightly jealous Prithwish, who belonged to an upper-class family from Dalton Ganj now settled in Kolkata. He always had a bit of superiority which he liked to display.

'Shows that books can't teach you everything' said the impish Arpan wanting to rub it in, he disliked Prithwish.

'It is just a start, let's see what happens,' Alekhya said modestly.

'Where are you going exactly?' asked Prithwish.

'South of Madurai. That is all I know for the moment. The professor had warned him not to disclose the full details, you never knew people was what he said, they got envious when you did something out of ordinary, something your peers had not done. There was danger in doing something extraordinary and specially in being perceived at doing so, which often counts for more in most cases. It was true as far as Alekhya's knowledge about human nature went.

'By flight?' asked Priya, opening her mouth for the first time while sipping the mocktail.

'Bagchi sir has done all the arrangements; he is going to inform me today.'

'Lucky you. We all drool after Bagchi sir and here he is taking you along to an archeological expedition.'

It is not all luck, smiled Alekhya wanly.

Whatever it is, we want a party when you are back and famous said Arpan, the others joined in unison.

Alekhya laughed 'ok we will see about that.'

Yes, and the booze will be double, three cheers for Alekhya and though the two others joined in there was no ring of truth in the cheers. A line of demarcation had been drawn in the mind, he had drawn ahead and was alone, a loneliness that is often a part of success.

***

'Our tickets are booked; we will be flying to Chennai and after a day there take the night express to Madurai.' The deep voice of the professor, at 7 in the evening finally told Alekhya of their travel plans.

He was too much in awe of the professor to ask more, he still felt intimidated by his great name and reputation. Bagchi was never known to seek others' opinions or look at what was convenient for them, it was his way or the highway for him. Alekhya came back in tizzy of excitement to his room and lay on his bed looking at the revolving ceiling fan, so it was final. They were going to the place indicated in the ancient manuscript, it was he, Alekhya a first year MA student of history who was the principal architect of this expedition. Bagchi of course had the hard bit, getting the logistics done but it was the original work that was responsible, he felt elated, on top of the world and his reverie was broken by the entry of the food plate borne by the mess staff.

He saw he had little time left to finish his packing. The flight tickets sent on his WhatsApp by the professor was the material proof.

***

The flight glided to a stop at the runway of Chennai international airport still known by its MAA from its old appellation of Madras to the world of flights. It was Alekhya's first time in a flight and he had been disillusioned, like many things that are too anticipated it had proven to be a disappointment. The check in, the glamour of the lounge and the security checks had made him anticipate, expect a different kind of excitement. But the plane once airborne, the takeoff had been nail-biting with its sound, speed, the rapidly vanishing trees, and buildings seen from the window to the sudden feeling of weightlessness as the plane became airborne and then there was nothing else.

The professor was not a great companion. Sullen, forbidding and domineering he sat absorbed in his own thoughts. It was evening in Chennai, hot and sultry as they came out and took a taxi to the hotel. The professor wanted to meet some officials next morning before starting for Madurai. The hotel they arrived at was surely a five star one Alekhya supposed though he had never seen one or knew how stars were given.

The swank grandeur was everywhere to be seen and felt. The room was huge, a smaller room with a refrigerator lead into a large lofty chamber. This was what a suite was. The hotel boy dropped Alekhya's luggage rather cavalierly in the anteroom and took the professor's luggage to the inner chamber.

***

Sreenivas T had tucked into his breakfast, a large portion of sambhar and idlis which were mashed into a mixture as the real Chennai people loved to have it. He had put in only a mouthful and savoring the taste, his wife was a good cook when the mobile rang. It was the deputy director as the contact's name showed. Disgusted but forced by hierarchy he somehow swiped the screen missing twice with his slightly greasy finger before picking up the call. He hated this priggish and dictatorial man.

'Yes sir, good morning.' Sreenivas's tone reverential almost obsequious.

The deputy director known to be an ill-tempered man ignored the good morning and came straight to the point. 'I need you in Chennai by tomorrow. You are to supervise a new site dig. Your order has been sent to

Kolkata office. Take the morning flight tomorrow,' the phone was disconnected.

The bosses never wanted what you wanted to do, whether there were any issues. Anything they needed at once had to be done.

Sreenivas was transported into a reverie as he absent-mindedly ate his remaining breakfast. On one hand this meant transfer albeit temporary to his native place, something he was desperately wanting and on the other hand was his last experience at the dig. The humiliation, the way he had been replaced, the inglorious way in which he had been transferred to the dinghy and sultry Kolkata.

The Vaigai valley had asked some impertinent questions and though the southerners were not too displeased with them the corridors in north had been provoked and with an election looming in a months' time, things had been brushed under a big carpet with a powerful broom and dust flies like him had been swept away to distant Kolkata. The dig had lost its way and meandered. Something must have happened to make the deputy director call himself, something big. So, he hoped but too much hope often led to disappointment, licking the last bit of sambhar from his bowl, he got up and went for his bath, he had to take his release order from the Kolkata office. At least he could escape from this place.

He seemed to feel the breeze of the Bay of Bengal blow on him as he came out of the bath wrapped in a towel after his shower, the mouthwatering idlis, the coconut trees…well Chennai is also known for its torrid heat, but we tend to remember only good things about our native places, memory is a selective thing… deceptive and often facultative.

Chapter 14

At a famous restaurant in uptown New York three people were seated at dinner. It was the special treat for one of them. He was travelling to India, the expedition being sponsored by none other than one of the great connoisseurs of south Asian culture, Mathew Pritchard, and his private museum of anthropology.

Martin Lahiri had been born in Tripura a backward, small hilly state in north eastern India and brought up in US. His real name was Sayantan though he had changed it when he was old enough to do it. When he had come to the United States of America at the age of thirteen years, he was of a ripe enough age not to forget his origin but he chose to do so in the fashion of his parents who had a great dislike for anything Indian. Though his surname suggested an Indian origin he was as far removed from it as possible, he tried to look and often succeeded a two generation American twice over he was more American than the Americans. He was the typical young American that one encounters at so many places. But from one side he was different, he loved studies of art and culture of various countries and his essay had won him the prize that permitted him a foreign trip for exploration sponsored by the Pritchard foundation. At 30, Lahiri had the world at his feet or so he felt.

His mother who had sporadic bursts of Bengal and Bengali sentiment had tried once to infuse him with a dose of Tagore which he had discarded without much delay. Many people who come from other countries do try this cultural infusion and in most cases it fails. A tree can grow up naturally only when it is cultivated in that environment.

His partner was an American photographer, Sam Hewett who also shared his love for the oriental art and culture. He unlike Sayantan, loved Indian culture, heritage, and its manifestations in myriad shades around the diverse country.

He was extremely excited to visit the country he had read about and seen videos of only till now.

The third person in the dinner was from the Pritchard foundation and was giving precise instructions as to their work once they had located the prehistoric dig, he seemed to be very professional, thorough, and mechanical. Sometimes these things go hand in hand.

***

The hotel they were staying in was in Anna Salai and it was one of those upmarket places. Coming out of the hotel it seemed tremendously hot to Alekhya, however Bagchi immediately hailed an auto, the

Chennai contraption with its canary yellow body and black roof, travelling through the crowded streets they reached Vanagram, not upmarket as Anna salai but the new built-up area, the one that is seen in almost all metropolis mushrooming out of the main city to accommodate a bulging population. The building in front of which the auto had stopped seemed like a government office complex. Taking the lift, they reached the fourth floor, where archeological survey was written in black upon an old brass plate. Alekhya understood the purport of coming here.

Professor Bagchi had told Alekhya little of his activities since coming here though he was not averse to taking every help that Alekhya had to offer. After a wait in the lobby decorated with sofas and a large centre table, the receptionist called the professor who went hurriedly asking curtly Alekhya to wait.

***

The direct train from Kottayam to Madurai had been the night express which arrived at Madurai at 10.40 am. The historian Rajeev Nair had got an upper berth in the 2 AC compartment, ensconced in his berth as soon as the train left Kottayam, book in hand, reading lamp on. It was the seat of his choice, the one you could get up at once and be least disturbed. There was another reason too, he snored. He tried his best to go to sleep last in the coach when several other co passengers were snoring too. He was a quiet and shy man and, in all matters, including this trivial physical problem he did not want to draw attention to himself.

The hard bound book was India, a history by John Keay and it was sometimes accompanied by a spiral bound note. A report on the Keeladi excavations by the government that had been undertaken some years back. He had been invited as he usually was by ASI officials of the neighboring state to help them when any new site was being excavated, a quiet scholarly man with huge practical experience of working in such sites in the country as well as abroad. He was not very rich and preferred a simple life and the government authorities liked him. He was there go-to man, a man they could trust. Bagchi for all his show of knowledge had not impressed them to be one to left unguarded. He needed a monitor who had more experience than him.

Chapter 15

The Chennai- Madurai express was to leave from platform no 4. It was crowded, hot and humid. The famous documentary maker with all his equipment loaded in a backpack and one sling bag was huffing and puffing on his way through the crowd. Chennai the land of films however did not recognize the world-renowned documentary maker, who saw documentaries when they were the Tamil blockbusters to see! Had it been even a minor star from the commercial films, the crowd would have lifted him up and garlanded him on way to his compartment.

The two-tier AC sleeper was clean. That was the first impression that Iyengar had on entering it. The trains were getting cleaner in India. This would be a topic of one of his future documentaries, trains in India-the largest network of railways in the world. He had his choice seat, a side lower berth. He was more apprehensive than happy till he could ensure that the seat remained his. Always there was the chance of it being appropriated by a person who was either old or ill asking for it. Iyengar could never refuse and often lost it.

Seated in the lower berth seat counting his stars, Iyengar took out the camera which had a large lens attachment, very impressive in appearance. Iyengar studied it intensely. It was not that the study was immediately required but like most humans had a natural urge to impress the opposite sex which had appeared in the coup in the form of two very beautiful young girls who were giggling at some secret joke.

Iyengar who had a good and sharp eye had already noticed that they were gazing blushingly at the famous documentary maker, he was a regular feature of many TV shows.

***

They were to stay at the hotel at Keeladi. It was quite a distance from the excavation site, twenty kilometers in fact but options were limited. It was a small town, more like a hybrid village which has received a dose of growth manure. There were no decent hotels. It was little matter to Alekhya but Bagchi was not happy. It was just a small one that would have qualified as a horsy inn in older times. There were just ten rooms and all of them were booked. Many of the people who were here for the dig were staying in homes of people now claiming to be homestays and charging as much as they could squeeze out. Human nature all around the world used to taking advantages was no different here. Nor was it anything novel.

Alekhya and the professor were to stay in the same room, not a very comfortable situation but nevertheless it was the circumstances that made strange bedfellows. Bagchi had heard from someone that power cuts were rather common and swarm of mosquitoes zeroed in on their target almost at once. He could be induced under no pretext to stay anywhere else but the small hotel which at least had an old-fashioned generator.

The likely excavation site had been identified the previous day and that day by following the directions given in the scripture. It hadn't been easy and would have been impossible without the interpretation of the writing, Alekhya should have had the credit for this but somehow, he found himself pushed to the sidelines. Bagchi who knew the details from Alekhya but had made careful notes from his basic interpretation made by his student and never referred to them while working from the notes, impressed all by his almost oracular reading of the directions. No one had any doubts as to the identity of the scripture reader. We believe what we see, often what we are made to see, by no means the same thing but often confused by a large populace, its very principle being at the heart of marketing.

***

A crowded south Indian restaurant was the first taste he had of the hot place, an unpleasant welcome. Alekhya, a Bankura boy had been only exposed to the food style in west Bengal and this had proved to be a cultural shock for him. He was now to subsist on this staple food for the remainder of his stay. Bagchi seemed immune to what he ate, he was too absorbed in his work. Alekhya hated the sambhar, rice and coconut oil flavored vegetables, an assortment of which was served in various little bowls of steel none of which it seemed to Alekhya tasted from one another. Only the thin water like rasam seemed a godsend, he could have that in plenty.

He had just had his lunch and was returning to the hotel when Bagchi called on his mobile, he was going out, the key was at the reception. No further details were given. Alekhya knew it meant the professor would have taken the vehicle with him and he was now to stay at the hotel till he returned therefore having no active role to play at the initial stage of this much touted expedition.

He ate a few bananas that he had purchased from a roadside shop and prepared to laze away the afternoon. Entering the hotel and getting the keys from the reception he went up to the room, turned on the TV and putting the fan on full speed lay on the bed. Soon he fell asleep.

***

Bagchi made it very clear to the archeological survey team right from the first that it was he who had the full quadrants to the site of the civilization they were here to discover. It was going to be near the Vagai river but a little more upstream. The location was to be about twenty-five miles from it but the factors to be considered was the fluvial plain that changed sometimes with the course of a river and the river had certainly changed its course over a few thousand years. Of course, he had much more accurate data due to the notes of Alekhya but that was not for now, it had to be gradually disclosed. Credit was thing that had to be taken in, people who are masters at it can do so quite easily.

Time and tide are said, wait for no one. It is a famous adage and not one to be taken lightly. Tide had changed the course of the river Vaigai and it was a narrow file of water, somewhere even stagnant like a cesspool. The scriptures had the descriptions of thousands of years back and rivers and forests had both disappeared from their original places. However, science had new tools, radars which could penetrate the ground., aerial survey gadgets. All the things that civilizations had created often lead to the vanishing of trees and rivers but the implements of civilization were good at bringing out their corpses.

The spot or location that could be made out from the markings of a small hill that seemed to stand still over the years was a five square kilometers area, a wasteland was a better word for absence of a stronger word that could aptly describe it. Alekhya had seen the process of zeroing in on the area, but to the naked eye, this place looked as unlikely to be the spot for development of civilization as thousands of years ago.

The searching of thirty square kilometers of area had been reduced to this place by the use of ground penetrating radar, subterranean structures had been heard. But it could turn out to be some modern foundation or structure till the excavations were done. Bagchi had been frantic and tried to convince the officials to start with this as it matched with the scriptures. The new IAS, secretary for art and culture in the state was heard to have been an engineer before she entered the civil services. She gave the nod and it is well known in India that the bureaucracy holds the key to any decision making. It certainly proved so here and it was decided to start the dig. It was rumored that the secretary herself would be visiting the site once something promising came to view. The funds were being released with much greater alacrity now once the bureaucratic assent had been obtained. Bagchi had played a key role here; his mesmerizing powers of the lectures being unleashed on the officials.

The place was to the south east of Madurai, a small hamlet little to the north of Keeladi. What was only a village in recent times, a backwater became the hub of activity.

The first day at the excavation site proved depressing for Alekhya. He had assumed that archeological digs would be exciting and fun but like most things in life when you do get down to that highly anticipated job it only proves itself mundane, often even drab, and boring.

There were large number of people but most to Alekhya's eyes seemed to be doing anything but talk, Bagchi being amongst them. After an hour of deliberation that resulted in the man with straw hat and loose-fitting white cotton shirt shouting to a group of men who were lounging below a clump of coconut trees. They came now armed with picks. Shovels and huge sized metallic tapes with which measurements began under the watchful eyes of a ruffianly looking man right out of the films. He seemed to know his job, cigarette in one hand and barking short precise orders to the labourers. Young impatient Alekhya thought it quite a puzzle as they marked out specific points using magnetometer by the superintendent, the ruffianly looking man.

Alekhya did not seem to exist for any of them. He was absolutely ignored. Bagchi was consulted by the officials sitting on a camp chair under the shade. He was the man with the knowledge, they knew it from grapevine that even the secretary had been impressed by his knowledge. People can often be made to believe various things; it is a technique one must master.

Chapter 16

Long flights are a big bore. Those who have travelled from the US to India or to China or from UK to the New Zealand or Australia would be able to relate immediately to the feeling. For those who haven't it's a new experience.

Since the flight had taken off from the JFK, he had seen three movies, listened to music, ordered two noodles in a cup and yet when he looked at his watch only two hours had gone by, nearly 15 hours were left. Just imagine sitting in that small space in the economy class seats having nothing to do, nothing to see, it was terrible. Sayantan made a promise, he would not make such long trips ever again, except to return of course to the US.

Sitting in that long flight from New York to Mumbai, he thought about all the things that he had to face in India, his parents had always given such negative vibes about the place that he could not thing anything positive about it, we are all tutored at some stage in our lives and the effect of the tutoring stays with us.

His partner was however oblivious to all these matters, he sat in his seat, front tray open, a mobile phone in airplane mode on in one hand from which he was intently studying something, taking only an occasional break to scribble furiously in a black hardbound notebook.

****

The paper had finally been accepted, not published. Not in a famous journal as Bagchi had expected but in a good one, double peer reviewed, it would stand as a testimony to their pioneering work in the field. Alekhya was there at number three. Bagchi was the first author and the second author was the assistant director of ASI. Alekhya knew about it beforehand as Bagchi had told him that no journal would accept a paper from a student, that required specialization. He had agreed naturally not knowing the process too well.

A publication in a journal is a big thing for an undergraduate student and he had agreed eagerly. Now he thought he understood the reason behind all this but the author contribution had been signed and it had been sealed. It was documentation no one could dispute. Bagchi was the undisputed author, the main one of the publications. The finding was his, the research was his too, he had led the team and would have lion's share of the credit too. That had been the wily professor's intention right from the start, though he would never have accepted it.

***

Priya had just returned from a birthday bash. She had missed Alekhya, but he was away as he had made her understand on the work of his life, their life maybe if things went as she planned. Her mother had made the customary payesh or rice pudding and had given her the money she needed to spend with her friends to keep her so called status amongst them. Now back home she felt the need to hug her, to make her feel special. But her room was closed. Lights turned off. A bit odd but then it was nearly 11.30, she had missed looking at the time in her urge to please her friends. She decided to call Alekhya and share her day, surely, he was waiting for her call. Too timid to call her during the party, though he had been one of the first to wish at twelve midnight yesterday, the time when people still young call to wish, when birthdays have not yet become the index of passing years, of age on the wrong side.

She had put the mobile on silent mode while at the night club and forgotten to put it back to sound mode. There were a few missed calls and a mail, from her mother. She was surprised. An email from her mother was the last thing she expected. She started reading forgetting all about the missed calls. There was no stopping reading this, it was a time bomb and it had exploded.

***

Mother and daughter were face to face. There are moments in life when you want to avoid the closest, the nearest and ones you love the most. It is a reaction, a certain respect to be retained, there is a certain respect in avoidance, not looking in the eye. The curtain when raised between a relationship is not always pretty to look at. Nakedness is revealing, but nakedness is also stark and often quite disturbing. One may have a desire to see it when prevented by once having seen, the veil is raised and leaves nothing but emptiness.

Priya was the first to blink, she turned and went into the open kitchen, put on the electric kettle, poured water, and switched it on. Her mother she heard had switched on the TV, the sound of the news channel always breaking news was on, it could be compared with the incessant breaking of waves.

She came out, bearing a cup of coffee, dark, strong smelt of burning. She sat down, almost slumped down on the sofa...both intent on seeing the TV screen, unseeing eyes seeing nothing.

It was Shreyashi who broke the silence.

'You could have made me a cup too...'

'Oh sorry, I did not think...she stopped mid-sentence. Leaving the sentence unfinished, it is often easier, we leave them unfinished when it is difficult to finish them.

She got up like an automaton while her mother held up her hand.

'Sit down, I do not need coffee. I need to talk.'

And out it came like torrents of gushing water, the water as if pent up for years inside a dam. A dam of patience, of motherhood and extreme level of tolerance.

Chapter 17

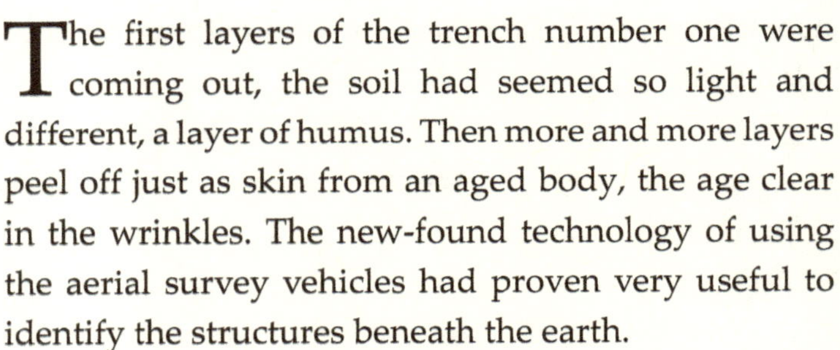

The first layers of the trench number one were coming out, the soil had seemed so light and different, a layer of humus. Then more and more layers peel off just as skin from an aged body, the age clear in the wrinkles. The new-found technology of using the aerial survey vehicles had proven very useful to identify the structures beneath the earth.

The pit had yielded some implements which were more like working people's it seemed not a race much for ornamentation. More of workhorses they seemed to have. Only interested in work and no play. These people Bagchi would have liked.

Alekhya knew about such people; his communism had prepared him for such people. The people who had belonged to this ancient civilization seemed just like that. They had no love for art or fine things in life without which life he thought was mundane.

The implements were of glass, paste, quartz, agate, cornelium, terracotta. Things one expected in an industrial civilization. So were these people just like that, hardworking, industrious, and not afraid of God or nature which often amounted to the same thing in earlier phases of civilization.

***

To grow up with one parent however good or caring was often like to stand anchored on the ground with only one skewed root, a weak anchor without the counterbalance. The plant lives on due to the nourishment it receives and thus fails to die, but its living in a skewed way, pulled one way while yearning for the other. Maybe death is better in some ways than living in this manner.

Till she had known that her mother had brought up her alone her father an unknown factor it was tolerable but now that she knew who the father was the distance had only grown more, was its physical distance?

She saw the man she had respected as a teacher grow indistinct and a man who was her father come out of the indistinct shadows, cruel, domineering, and selfish. It was hateful to think of it, she herself full of righteous anger.

Chapter 18

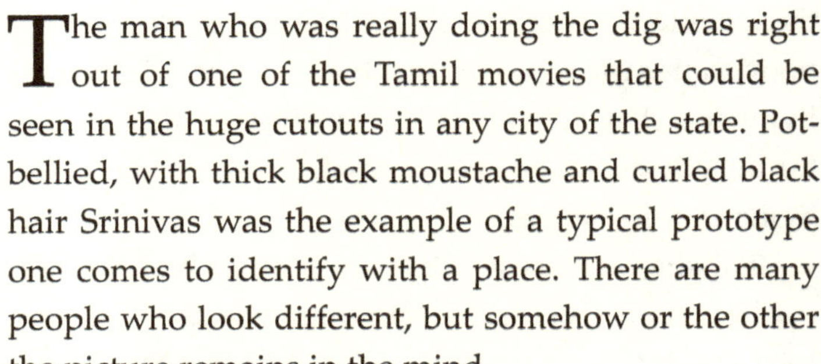

The man who was really doing the dig was right out of one of the Tamil movies that could be seen in the huge cutouts in any city of the state. Potbellied, with thick black moustache and curled black hair Srinivas was the example of a typical prototype one comes to identify with a place. There are many people who look different, but somehow or the other the picture remains in the mind.

He was the life of the dig, doing things with his own hand, shouting, and pulling with the labourers when any heavy task presented itself, he was the type that Alekhya loved. The ones who did it themselves rather than directed others to do things.

Bagchi was usually seated at the makeshift tent with the higher ASI officials and the documentary maker, the American team members mostly being absent till some specific news of a dig being completed or something being discovered went to them through the numerous people they had bribed to get such information, preferring the cool shade of the hotel room to the scorching sun that is so typical of this place.

Srinivas, however went on like an automaton only stopping occasionally to puff a cigarette behind the coconut trees. It was there that Alekhya caught up with him. He smiled showing a set of yellowed teeth, and offered Alekhya a cigarette.

'Do not you think that I am going to get any credit for all this work. It's all going to go to them.' He pointed a thumb in the direction of his bosses' camp. 'The last time not even my name appeared in the papers. It is just that I love our culture, am proud of it and want to discover it with my own hands.'

'But that is unfair…you should get the credit. If only for your part.' Alekhya had all the righteousness perfect for his stage of life.

Srinivas smiled, a sad smile. 'The world is not fair, it is cruel. You will know it one day, all of us does.'

***

One who has seen an archeological excavation site with a layman's eye will not be impressed. Layer after layer of soil and debris coming out creating a cavity, the sort you see while buildings are made for laying foundations. However, to the trained expert they open a vista of possibilities, layers of history unfolding in front of eyes. Alekhya had been disillusioned while Bagchi and Nair with the ASI officials were all excitement. All the things that had come to light from this excavation till now had pointed to this being a civilization of artisans, of hard-working men and women, signs of early industrialization, the type that believes in all work no play. A bit boring but the type that a developed nation probably would aspire to be, people not given to art or debauchery or pleasantries. Alekhya observed the things from a distance, a bemused spectator. After some time scrolling through his mobile, his friends were having a party, lots of photos from the part and even a video was on the social sites, bored with the proceedings, he left the site and walked to the tea shop. Life sometimes was so tedious, he felt. Here he was half ignored, half-forgotten watching a prehistoric site, he suddenly felt the excitement ebb out of him like a receding tide, sudden and leaving a tired waste behind.

Chapter 19

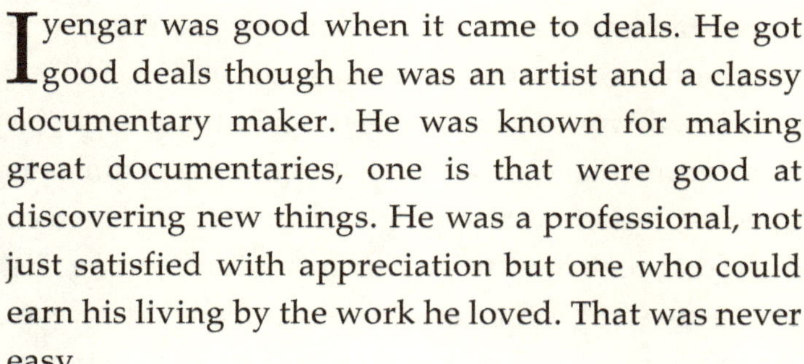

Iyengar was good when it came to deals. He got good deals though he was an artist and a classy documentary maker. He was known for making great documentaries, one is that were good at discovering new things. He was a professional, not just satisfied with appreciation but one who could earn his living by the work he loved. That was never easy.

So, he had his eye on the business side of things while he practiced his art. It was not for nothing that the documentary maker had made a goodly fortune from his documentaries. He had struck the nail at the right moment here too. He had been able to sell off the rights of the excavation to the American museum representatives, the Indian American had thought himself too smart and Iyengar was good at exploiting these weaknesses.

He had mainly focused on work of the Kolkata professor, Bagchi. Made him out to be the hero of this find just like RD Banerjee, in IVC. The right hinges needed to be oiled if the door of success must be unlocked, no point in being over scrupulous in these matters, Iyengar for one never suffered from that malady, yes, it is a malady; conscience.

He made it Bagchi's work, his great discovery. The scripture from an old specimen of Sangam literature discovered while he was visiting his student's home, a remote village in the district of Bankura. He had understood the importance of the scripture, its understanding that matters, there are many things one sees with one's eyes, what you need is vision.

He was working hard on getting the things right for this documentary, he knew that lighting of a film was often as important as the film itself. A realistic effect, often different from the commercial film lighting. He was a master as that art, he remembered the years of training and effort it had taken. An excavation in southern India that was a new phase in the Indian civilization could attract an international audience like most of his documentaries did, awards a little controversy and the fame that comes with it. Iyengar knew the potential of this work.

An international recognition could come, the coveted awards. Well, it was not for nothing that Iyengar always did his research properly. One needed to be prepared if one is to get the maximum out of a project, Iyengar was an old hand at it.

***

Dr. Nair was a well-known professor of history and had worked with the ASI on several excavations. He was the ASI's man in the team. They needed him to vouch for the finding that Bagchi was giving them. Bagchi had theoretical knowledge but little experience of handling expeditions. Nair was the man to lead or at least control the dig from the ASI side. He was silent, soft-spoken man who seldom spoke when it could be avoided. Nair had got on with Bagchi, not surprising as Nair could really get on with anyone. It was what you could call his USP or unique selling point, people like product had to sell; that is the most important quality whatever else you bring to the table is an addition.

He had kept a hawk's eye on the proceedings and reported every little detail to the people who mattered. So, what was happening on the dig, what the findings exactly were, the bosses knew well in advance of the official report that was to be submitted by Bagchi, who was hardly aware of the mole right beneath his nose. Nair was good at his work, avoided stepping on anyone's shoes and silently did his job. An efficient, well-oiled machine, it was not for nothing that his employers trusted him. Not everything in history is palatable, not everything can be served. It had to curated, customized, and then presented. Researchers and professors were usually over enthusiastic, the society or better to say the political bosses could not always respond in the same vein, it could be troublesome, some sleeping dogs were best kept that way.

He was good at the practical side of the job too, which Bagchi lacked. He was fluent in the local language, knew the geography of the place and it was his silent efforts that was leading to the rapid unearthing of many things that otherwise would have taken much greater time, though Bagchi was loathe to accept it; we seldom are open to giving credit where it is due unless magnanimous and Bagchi's best friend could not have called him that even if were a eulogy. Nair however did not seem to mind. He was engrossed in his work, with his field notebook, hat and clad in linen shirt always working together with the labourers who did the heavy work. Alekhya who had initially ignored him now was quite attached to him. Though he was not garrulous afraid of upsetting Nair but he put in a question from time to time on the practical aspects of archeology as he saw it on the site and was delighted that the quiet man answered him in measured tones but never ignored him; something that his own professor was often doing now.

Chapter 20

The findings of the site signified clearly two things, one that an urban settlement had flourished in the south along with the Harapan civilization and the Indus valley as described in the scripture, a part of the Sangam literature and second it was clear that this was an industrial civilization, literate which shared a close bond and trade relations with the various regions of the country and the world. The inscriptions on all the pottery and tablets bore similar symbols of the language often seen in the Indus valley objects. The sharing of common words and signs could now be cited as a definitive proof that there had been no north to south migration as was often claimed, the civilizations in the north preceding those in the south by several hundred years. It was now clear that even south to north migration had occurred. Borrowing of words taken place from the south by the Indus valley people clearly showed that.

Alekhya was delighted. His correct reading of the ancient Sangam script had all lead to this, the discovery of a new site, the carbon dating reports once they came from the earth science laboratory in the university of Pisa would be the final proof, he a student in his twenties would become famous, a new archeologist whom the world would reckon. He had written it all down in his notebook. His professor had of course organized the whole thing with the archeology department, it was more logistic activity in his view, he was yet to realize that this was no less difficult in a country where funds and funds for research were not easy to obtain, but he was the one with the discovery. Had he not read the scripture and understood it correctly, the civilization would have laid buried under the soil, as it had done for thousands of years.

He walked head held a little high or was it his imagination above the common man, he was uncommon amongst them, a rare breed. He had not seen Bagchi for some hours, he had not heard from the officials too as to the time of leaving the dig for the day. Somewhat mortified, he took an auto which charged him more than usual to the hotel.

One who has never seen a human body from inside is often excited at the prospect of seeing it dissected in front of the eyes, however it often proves a disappointing experience for most. The same was true for excavations Alekhya felt after spending all these days on the dig. Digging deep into the body of the earth is often non-promising for all except the trained archeologist who finds the pages of history seen in the shreds of broken things, potteries, half tiles with inscriptions bearing testimony to the civilizations who have now been reduced to dust. We all are reduced to the same stage one day but till that day arrives we live in oblivion of the fact; a trained oblivion essential to existence and life.

***

Today things at the excavation were proceeding with an almost too beautiful mechanical grace. It could be called almost created to please the eye, so it was. Nothing in life is usually without reason nor was this. It was the day of the secretary's visit with her usual entourage to the site. Civil servants, after politicians get the greatest importance in the country. They are the ones with the decision-making power, they are all powerful in a system where, knowing something of everything is considered to outweigh knowing everything of something. Thus Geetanjali Sharma, engineer turned IAS of the Tamil Nadu cadre was the go-to person in this case. Another legacy that the civil services, no means an easy exam though a little too heavy weather is made of it is that they usually have a huge entourage, security, pilot cars as if one had any real need to know them much less harm, but it lent an importance in the eyes of the public thus exalting it to heights that went with these offices.

Geetanjali had passed out of one of the top engineering universities in the city and then tiring of corporate world had decided to appear in civil services exam. Her cadre did not please her as she had been forced to move out of her native Jaipur to the southern state but one cannot have everything in life, she at least understood that. She had adjusted and now was heading the art and culture department of this extremely culturally rich state. After her visit which involved a lot of protocols and security was over, people at the site heaved a sigh of relief. Things were back to normal.

Bagchi had been her chief guide to the relics found from the excavation. She had probably been affected by his charm and knowledge whereas silent Nair had not cut much ice with his dour looks and silence. Bagchi had the gift of the gab and the ASI officials thought it better to let him do the talking and answer the questions she had to ask of them. Alekhya who saw all of this from a distance as there was heavy security and he could not venture very close to bureaucracy got most of it second hand later from Sreenivasan.

It all took a couple of hours. Knowing something of everything IAS officers had this innate ability to assimilate quickly in hours what others could do in days, months or often years. That was what made them different, no wonder the government spent lavishly on them and depended on them to run the government. In this case the work earned her approval.

***

Priya was travelling by a crowded metro train from the station near her home, an auto ride of ten fifteen minutes to her college near Central metro station. A small child and her mother seemed to be taking the train to a school quite far away from home, the uniform was that of a reputed school in south Kolkata, the one from which she herself had passed. The mother had sad eyes; a fact Priya could now recognize. She smiled wanly at her daughter who seemed oblivious to the fact. She wanted to cover it up perhaps, give the child hope. There was certainly hope when you travelled from the extreme north of the city to the south in hope of giving good education, just like her mother had done, was doing. Hope was something that kept people going when all else was gone. Hope of education, hope of employment and hope of the illusionary empowerment that the government always talked about.

Was really getting a good education the key to employment, not always as the recent scams at various employments had proven. Faces with grief, faces with hopelessness that lined the city streets; she could not dwell further on these thoughts. She was already in an agony, she had to get over negative thoughts. The train was slowing down, the next station was hers.

The mother-child duo was still sitting. They had still a long way to go. Priya got up; a queue had already formed inside the train for the commuters who were going to get down. Faces; unknown, tired, hopelessness, sadness, and yes inscrutable faces.

Chapter 21

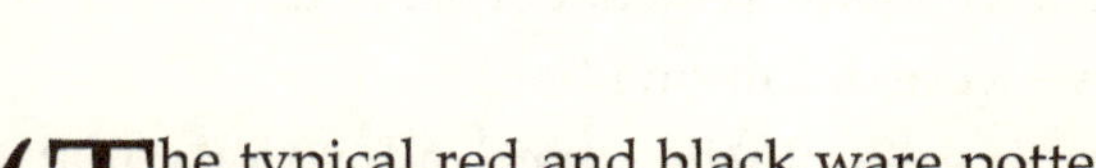

'The typical red and black ware pottery that was found yesterday, it's a classic example,' the professor's eyes were shining behind his round large glasses. 'It shows that the artisans knew the technique of raising the kiln temperature to 1100 degrees Celsius.'

'Hmm, I think you are right. Do you remember the results of the spectroscopic analysis of the black and red ware by the earth science department at Pisa?'

'You bet I do, of course. It is the same, hematite for red and carbon for black. Just send this for analysis and see the results.'

'Well, it seems they were a civilization of artisans' sort of craftsmen…they'

Someone was knocking at the door.

The professor got up and opened it with a dour face. Alekhya

'Yes, what do you want' he asked shortly.

'Sir. I have something to discuss with you.'

Not now. I am busy. You see the deputy director is here. We are discussing important things.

'But it was I…'

'Whatever you want to say we will talk about it later. Now go out and enjoy the market.'

The door was slammed shut in Alekhya's face.

'Who was it? Wasn't that your student?'

'Pestering brat. These guys are very good at taking a mile if you give them an inch. Forget it. Let us get on with what we were discussing.'

'Ah yes, these people they were industrious, that's what I was telling.'

'Hmm yes,' the professor looked a little distracted.

'And the pottery shreds, the letters engraved on them, it shows a high level of literacy in early 6th century BCE.'

'Iyengar is coming. I have called him at 2 pm. Will you speak to him.'

'Yes, we need to come to an adjustment. Where is the US team now?'

'They have gone to see the dig, said they wanted some samples of the walls, the construction materials. They want to get them analyzed at Vellore.'

'It has got silica, lime etc. the same we had in Keeladi, just see how long they have survived, that will give you an idea of the material used.'

'Right, now let us grab some lunch. They will be waiting for us. I do not want the US guys here.'

'Ok, let us have a South Indian thali.'

The professor picked up the intercom and dialed room service. His face was inscrutable, like a mask.

Chapter 22

It was the day of the final pack up. The officials looking to make most of the weekend had left on the Friday morning as soon as it was light, the Friday would now count as a working day though they were using it to travel home and they could enjoy an extended weekend.

The US team was leaving too, waving their hands at anyone who cared to see or wave back at them. Alekhya watched this from his balcony, which was right on the main road which people travelling from that part of the town outwards bound were bound to take.

They had got what had been their objective all along, they had the first-hand experience of working in a dig, had been given that special treatment as Americans is used to in most places around the globe by dint of their nationality and had the samples they could put up at the museum and have analyzed to publish their findings in a reputed journal. Their mission was complete.

Alekhya before this exposure had never met foreigners from any place and his heightened idea of

America and Americans, built up by the imagery and propaganda, yes that was the correct word he thought bitterly was dashed. He had realized albeit to some extent that people were all the same everywhere. It is a reality that people often do not realize or even if they do, accept even when they had spent most of their lives and to realize this while still young was somewhat of a jolt, a veil drawn away from the illusions that often keep us happy. Sometimes it is better that they stay, they help us in our hours of gloom. Well, it had been removed and Alekhya felt a despondency that he had to fight now with all those fights he needed to do anyways.

Their train departure time was approaching too and in a couple of hours he would be journeying back with the professor, how different was this journey from the one he had done. He had undertaken this with him on a very different view to what he had now.

However, the bags had to be packed and though he was in no mood to eat he bought some bananas from a roadside vendor and absent mindedly munched on them as he went back to the hotel.

Chapter 23

The physical barrier of the curtains in the 2 AC coach seemed to Alekhya, a comfort, a comfort from the man he now seemed to draw himself away from. Even the gaze of the man had power to disturb him he felt.

He could not forget the words or the gesture of the man he had respected just after the lunch plates had been served. The supreme indifference that seemed to be more than any rebuke that he could have got. Professor Bagchi had been too engrossed in first scrolling the mobile and then furiously typing on the laptop. Alekhya had been absent to him for all purposes.

'Have you seen the pottery shreds Alekhya?'

'Yes sir, they showed me the photographs, some of them that is, enlarged.' His voice cool and tone dry.

The professor was too engrossed to notice them. These were small things and a great man like him did not notice small things. You could not become great if you noticed small things.

'Well, I have seen the originals, we are onto something big here if Dr. Nair here has agreed with me. They are the same type of black and red pottery found in the Indus and the inscriptions are similar too.' He rubbed his hands, eyes shining behind his big glasses.

Alekhya was downcast. He had certainly noted the 'we', He knew more than anyone else how the professor had no role in locating this archeological site. His correct reading of the inscriptions in the scripture with help from Duttagupta had led them to the place or close to it. Bagchi had only arranged the logistics part, the funding, but that was where his contribution ended.

But from what Alekhya had seen over the past few days, Bagchi had convinced everyone from the officials to the workers that it he the great professor who had found it all out after a student had come to him for help with deciphering the scripture found in their old family temple, he the acknowledged and well-known expert of ancient civilizations. Bagchi just like his classes had done it very convincingly. The publication was there with Bagchi as the first author and in allowing a mere student to be co-author for the published paper on the topic, he had indeed proven his magnanimity, a man who could be given that rare epithet of having a golden heart.

The professor was scribbling ferociously when his phone rang. As he went out of the compartment to the passage near the washrooms to get a better signal, Alekhya kept his gaze fixed on the vanishing trees and houses through the glass window, they were rapidly vanishing but not faster than his dreams…dreams when they vanish leave ruins, very sad ruins.

***

In Chennai, this time they had been allotted different rooms. Alekhya was relieved. He did not want to stay with this man, people who take away credit of others could not be tolerated, much less respected. He had lost the respect he had for the man, a continuous flow of events like sheets of rain had washed off the sheen of the man he had seen in Kolkata.

He had a small room on the ground floor, but at least he was separate. In the privacy of his room, he first dialed his mother's number, a change from his routine of last few months. He once again seemed to need the protection of the womb. Having told him of his arrival in Chennai, a fact that seemed to relieve her from the tone of her voice he told he would be returning to Kolkata in a couple of days and then to his village as soon as he was free of this project work. He felt lonely and he felt a longing for his own home that he had not felt over the past few months. They seemed to pass like a mirage in front of his eyes, non-existent now.

Then he called Priya, it had been tough calling him from the rooms he had been staying in. The professor was a difficult man to be comfortable with, he would not have asked who he was calling but those eyes would have bored into him like a X ray machine, seeing the very inside of him.

Today lying with his chest on the pillow, from the coolness of his room, the AC running at 20 degrees, he called Priya. His body was in comfort but his mind was exactly the opposite.

'You know what I am up against? The man is taking away all my credit. He is being touted as the person to have deciphered the script leading to excavation at this place, a new civilization as old as the IVC, the pottery shreds I told you about have gone to the labs at Pisa. Once the report comes, its expected soon, in a day or so it is going to be officially announced. His voice shook from excitement and apprehension.'

She had listened to the same recital day after day, again and again. Till today she had quietly listened. The words had varied slightly but the premise had remained the same. Gradually the words formed themselves, it had taken days of decision making and courage.

'What else do you expect Alekhya from a man who has deserted his wife and only child? What you say does not surprise me the least, it has not over the past two weeks.'

'What do you mean?' Alekhya was stumped. He had not known about Bagchi's personal life but for that matter how did Priya know it? And over the past two weeks!

'I mean that you have always wanted to know about my father, you have never mentioned it but you have always wanted to know, don't deny it now. Well Bagchi is the father I have never mentioned, not because I did not want to but because I never knew, till my birthday which was two weeks back. It was my 18th and my mother thought me fit enough to know now, an adult, she said.' She laughed, a harsh laughter that resounded in the ears.

'They were in university together, my mother and this man. My mother stood first and he was second when the results came out. He showed the greatest love and admiration for her, manipulated it in such a way to win her heart, making her pregnant, she had to marry him. She would have anyways but not in a hurry these circumstances made her do. In a weeks' time they were married and she awoke to the real character of the person she had married. There was a university lecturer post to be advertised soon. He forced her to forego the application on the ground she was pregnant. That was the start, the first step, the absence of the university topper leading to the second topper being selected. The first step on the ladder he has taken putting his foot on others.' Her voice was choked, with anger, with emotion and with the sadness of irreparable loss.

Alekhya could feel it in his body…

'What happened after that?'

Then he learnt it all, the surface was gone and the skeleton remained.

***

Bagchi was busy in his room, a large suite, a drink on the table. He was drafting the report of the dig to be signed soon by the other historian, the officials, and the ASI representative before being put before the government authorities.

He had been a bit worried since that call had come during the train journey. He had been asked to report to the Delhi offices after meeting some officials in Chennai in the evening. A car was to pick him up from the hotel. His whereabouts were not to be disclosed to anyone till he was instructed. It was the clandestine nature of the whole enterprise that worried him, what had happened to warrant such secrecy? He did follow the instructions; he could not do otherwise. For a start he had checked into a separate suite and allowed Alekhya to take a smaller room on his own. A room-mate is bound to be informed to some degree about the movements.

At 8 pm as he had been directed, he went to the hotel foyer, he did not have to wait as the car was waiting for him. Swiftly it bore him away through the lighted streets and then onto the darker outskirts of Chennai till he found himself at an isolated cottage, sea waves heard crashing outside. He was asked to sit by the security guards and almost immediately the inner door opened to admit three people, two of them well known to him.

***

A few words and the report had been altered; it had taken on a whole new shape. It is often said that history is written to the liking of the rulers of the state and often might have no relation to the truth. It is a fact that was close to the bone as the incidents had shown. History could be written, rewritten, or was written. Afterall, the people who write the history are in the service or patronage of the rulers. It could be tin pot god in form of a petty king earlier or the government now but people could be controlled with allurements or punished as the case might be, but they could be controlled.

It all suddenly seemed so easy, all read matters useless and puerile. Nothing had been written in history that was without bias. People didn't change, most still looked to appease the ruler.

Alekhya could hear the words of Bagchi echoing in his ears

'I will change the course of history and don't you dare cross me.'

A hand was near his throat, chocking the life out of him.

Alekhya awoke in cold sweat...he had been dreaming or was it true? He must have fallen asleep or was it some sort of premonition.

He went to Bagchi's room. No response. Surely at 11 in the night Bagchi could not have gone out!

He went down to the reception, suite no 407. No response. No keys with the reception either. This was a puzzle.

***

A call on his mobile early next day awakened Alekhya. It was Bagchi.

'I have some work for you. Come to my room.'

Brusque, arrogant, self-centered. All these words came to Alekhya's mind. He went to the lift after washing up and having his breakfast in the hotel dining room, as slowly as possible, taking maximum possible time. He had no wish to appease the man any further.

Bagchi seemed irked by the delay. He did not say so but his attitude showed it more clearly than words could express.

'Go through this document, just the spellings and typos. I have broken my reading glasses. Here is your ticket.' He handed a train ticket to Alekhya. 'Your train leaves in three hours, so be quick about it.'

Chapter 24

'What you are doing is positively criminal,' Alekhya had summoned up his courage to say this much and after a lot of practice. To face up to the famous and much senior man was not easy. He did not know what gave him the courage. Probably pushed to the wall he had been goaded into action. Even the gentlest of animals goaded to the limit sometimes show a resilience that often surprises the attacker or hunter.

'What you are doing is distorting history, you are no less than a criminal.'

Bagchi looked at him, without his glasses which he had broken. They were malevolent eyes. Then he smiled, a dangerous reptilian smile.

'Well history has always been like this, written to suit the powerful. It is not a novel crime if it is one at all. You are naïve, very naïve. Never thought that you were such a fool!'

'But my reading of the scripture, the discovery of the civilization, the dating of the articles…it could have changed the way people are used to thinking in our country. The hegemony probably could have been broken.'

'And what good it can it do? The government of the country could have been troubled; all the findings would have been questioned and led to formation of a government formed commission who would have rubbished all our findings and the report suppressed and never probably see the light of the day.'

Alekhya stammered 'we could have brought out the truth in a paper, published in a journal of repute.'

'You are too naïve, would the journal have published without proof, the dating of articles reports is with the ASI, a government body. We have no proofs. It is not a public document.'

'The documentary maker…'

Without permission of the authorities, he could not access the original proofs, he has just the pictures which can never prove the dates.'

'So, all the efforts are wasted.' Alekhya's voice shook with emotion.

'Read the rest of the report, see to the spellings. It's not quite so bad as you think, we will disclose the discovery of a new civilization, just push back the dates by a couple of centuries and the rest stays. You don't have much time for your train. Go on and highlight the things. Rest I will take care. Do not cross me Alekhya, it is not going to get you anywhere.'

There was quiet menace in the words which struck a chill, much more than the rowdy aggressive words of a ruffian could have struck to his heart.

***

The Chennai Santragachi AC special was slightly delayed. Alekhya was seated in the AC 3 tier despondent, his mood down. The professor's change had shocked him, the man he had respected almost revered was no longer there. He had been replaced by a double it seemed or was it that his mask had been removed, it was this that the original Bagchi was, what he had seen was only the veneer.

The inbound journey was as different to the outward journey as it could be, it was the mood that made it so different, while there had been excitement, hope and a challenge while travelling to the Chennai, it was despondency, disappointment, and disillusionment mixed with cynicism. It seemed to Alekhya that he had aged over the period of the weeks he had spent here. He yearned for home, the shades of the trees in his village and his mother. Gone were the days when he forgot to call or missed her calls, he just hoped to be back and lay his head on the lap of his mother, the door of the AC coach, the inner door of the compartment opened.

A beggar had come into the compartment with a small harp, the train was yet to start, soft musical tunes came to his ears and though he did not understand the language, the music fell softly on the ears and more soothingly on his mind, the magic that only music can do. He felt a little calmer and thought about what he had witnessed, in the finding of that scripture, his reading of it helped on by the brilliant but lazy Duttagupta and the usurping of the finished material by Bagchi. Was life always as unfair, he was too young and inexperienced to know but even if all of it had culminated in the true depiction of the civilization, he could have tolerated it to a degree, but now this changed report…it changed the context of the entire work. It made it much less important that it would otherwise be.

The beggar had disappeared and a young slim girl was asking him if he could please take the side upper berth, would he really mind? He could have answered that nothing seemed to matter any longer to him.

He just nodded his head, yes it was fine he said.

The train started with a slight lurch, something that happened with these modern coaches Alekhya had noted while travelling earlier.

***

He arrived at the boarding house after the long train journey, fatigued and disappointed. These are moments when one hopes to meet no one and be with oneself, unfortunately often fate decides differently.

It was the boarding's landlady's dog's birthday. The boarding house was decked up in coloured ribbons, its old plaster and dull whitewash quite in contrast to the brightly coloured ribbons. His roommate welcomed him with a huge cheer as soon as he entered.

Alekhya tried to put on a smile, it was not easy when inwards he was feeling a deep sense of disappointment. But we all can act even if was moments or for life, it's a quality that all of us possess if we care to explore it, people rarely do self-exploration, its painful and often undesirable to all of us.

'Well, here's the archeologist back from the hunt? How much gold was there or there was nothing in the hole?' He guffawed at his own joke.

Alekhya smiled. A wan smile. No there had been no gold.

'We are all dying to hear of your experience. No not now, after the grand dinner of the dog's birthday party.'

Alekhya nodded as he put the luggage in the corner and took his towel, soap, and bucket. He needed a shower badly. It was stifling, hot and humid and he had had no bath in the train for more than twenty-four hours.

***

It was now getting on to 2 am, the streets finally silent, vacant, and deserted. A drunkard was shouting abuses below, the echo resonating from the walls of all the age-old buildings that had also borne witness to such abuses. This area had been notorious since times immemorial.

His roommate was snoring loudly oblivious to all disturbances. It was always good to be insensitive, it saved you much trouble in the world. Not three hours ago was he boisterously laughing at Alekhya's discomfiture. Alekhya had been requested to recite his adventures by none other than the presiding deity of the boarding, the landlady herself after the special dinner in honour of Santa, her spaniel had finished. The chicken had been very spicy and the pulao rice hard. It had been departure at least from the routine rice, dal, and fish curry whose gravy was often like water.

Alekhya was still wide awake, sweat trickling down his forehead, the fan spinning overhead did nothing to dispel the heat or the sultry air than came in through the only window.

There was sense of loss, something akin to despair at his own helplessness. One never records one's exact feelings before death, was he going to take his own life? The ceiling fan seemed so alluring that he was attracted to it like a magnet.

***

Conclusion

The professor was delighted. The award ceremony had gone well. It had all been rehearsed and choreographed and Bagchi who was good at giving appearances had followed it to the letter. He had now received one of the high civilian honors the state had to offer. He was interviewed by news channels, print media reporters. He was the toast of the media, he had got what he had lacked till now, fame.

The next day's news papers were full of news of the now famous archeological excavations that had finally settled the question of the superiority of the races, so to say. Now there would not be any objection now to a Rastrabhasa or national language, a unified language that could be used across the country. The report of the archeological dig was there to support the claim. The government was happy. So were many people who had taken such a superiority to be granted but now had history behind them.

The inner pages, page eight to be precise, a small column on the left-hand side had another news. A young man aged about twenty-two had been found hanging from his room ceiling in the morning in a central Kolkata boarding house. The body was being sent for autopsy but the police had ruled out foul play, it was from the circumstances a simple open and shut case of suicide.

A bell was ringing, loudly. Did the police or someone else consider him involved in the case. Yes, abetment of suicide was a dangerous offence that demanded through investigation. That doddering old man must have lodged complaint. He tried to get up, something was holding him down. Something strong and supple...he woke up from sleep...looked around the room. Nothing had changed, it was time to go the college. He must have been dreaming...the world does not change quite so easily, there are innumerable reports to prove it. They have ended up where they were safest, in the shredder and then the dustbin. He had been dreaming.

Epilogue

Alekhya after staring at the fan in the dead of the night for an hour had seen something in the inner eye that as Wordsworth the poet had once said was the bliss of solitude. Though he was not exactly in solitude, he was in the company of a snoring roommate some two feet away, he was alone in the darkness, the darkness that often gives cover to our faults and covers our blemishes. He saw in that mind's eye the face of his mother and his doddering grandfather; they had brought him up fighting all hardships. They had not chosen the easy way out which is open to anyone who dares, or rather one who is afraid to face life. He could not bear to see pity for him and his family in the eye of others.

Life was like this for most, didn't he see thousands of such faces every day, didn't he know there were hordes of talented people in the world? They had failed to achieve fame but were no worse for it.

They could still live, be with their families and be even happy with small pleasures that life had to occur. He had once seen a blind man say to another, they felt they could laugh in each other's company, there was no one to pity them. Pity is the worst fate that can befall a man. He was now going to work for his studies, be a hardworking breadwinner for his family.

What if he did not have fame or a huge following, these things mattered but not always, they were not everything. It was getting light outside. Dawn was coming. Taking his bucket and mug from under his bed he opened the door and went to the bathrooms of the mess, still in sleep. Today there was no queue, he was early. It was the same everywhere. Proverbs did not lie; they were wise who had made them.

End

www.ingramcontent.com/pod-product-compliance
Lightning Source LLC
Chambersburg PA
CBHW022012150726
47990CB00002B/621